Professor David Bra[illegible]
*1955 - 2016*

*A wonderful friend and a brilliant scholar*

*Nothing is but what is not*

MACBETH ACT I, SCENE III

# THE SOHO INSTITUTE

Robbie J Robertson

**Three Wolves Publishing**

The characters and events portrayed in this book are fictitious. Any similarity to real persons, living or dead, is coincidental and not intended by the author.



ISBN-13: 9798580932163
ISBN-10: 1477123456

Cover design by: Jamie Robertson
Library of Congress Control Number: 2018675309
Printed in the United States of America

# CONTENTS

# CHAPTER 1 BRAVE NEW WORLD

The sun beat down steadily on the rooftops of Summertown and the air was still and solid. The sluggish summer atmosphere made movement heavy, and along the Woodstock Road cyclists sweated and squinted against the sun. In the colleges, porters sat back in their lodges, and took time to read the papers. No undergraduates for another month. Only the occasional tourist to disturb the tranquillity of the quads and chapels.

And as they turned the pages backwards from the crosswords and the sporting news, they read about a world so far removed from the suspended animation of their own, that it could have been a world in an entirely different universe. An enquiry had begun into the riots in Moss Side. A tenth IRA hunger striker was dying, slowly. A double murderer was on the run from Broadmoor. And beyond our shores President Reagan had commissioned the production of a neutron bomb. A fundraising event in New York had raised the profile of a new and worrying disease called AIDS, and further away still, over two million refugees were fleeing their homes in Afghanistan as the invading Soviet forces waged war.

But in the terraces and gardens of Summertown all was peace and tranquility. And in one particularly overgrown and chaotic garden, two friends sat reading, their minds focused on their studies, and detached from the world's headlines.

James Gunn reclined almost horizontality on the battered deckchair, his bottom inches from the ground. David Lawrence sat awkwardly in the discarded old armchair, carefully avoiding the springs which protruded through the cracked leather like alien tentacles. What had once been a lawn now resembled a small hayfield. The only sounds were those of flies investigating the dregs of the teapot and the cups which lay strewn amongst the grass, and the occasional thrum of a bus on the Banbury Road.

James glanced at Dave over his notes, as he lounged back in the moth-eaten chair.

'Are you going to meet your chapter deadline?' he asked.

'You know, I don't really have any choice, Jamie', replied Dave. 'My grant's running out, but I start teaching next month. I can't really study and work at the same time so the Huxley section has to be finished soon, and after that the thesis will be more or less complete.'

James stood up and stretched his arms to the sky which formed a perfectly blue canopy over the

Summertown terraces. His six foot frame was clad in a crumpled evening shirt, ancient khaki shorts, no socks and his size eleven brogues.

'What about you?', Dave asked, pouring the last few drops of tea from a chipped blue teapot. 'I'm happy that I'm staying here to teach. Don't you have any regrets about not staying on after your masters degree? I mean, what's the alternative? You can knock our rarified existence all you like, but the world outside is a complete bloody mess. Rioting in the streets, industries closing, political parties falling apart, ten percent unemployment. Even my favourite Doctor Who has been transmogrified! What have we got to cheer us up? Chariots of Fire, Bucks Fizz and a royal wedding. You know I'm an eternal optimist Jamie, but what are you actually going to do with yourself?'

James lowered himself carefully back into the creaking deckchair.

'Well, everything's a bit uncertain, but I'm hoping that something positive will come out of my meeting with Haldane tomorrow.'

James tried to stretch out and relax a little, the deckchair groaning ominously under his weight.

'I was actually getting fairly desperate until he took me aside during Eights Week. He asked me how my plans were going and so I told him about the endless applications, and the distinct lack of any replies. So then he pretty much assured me of a research job in some outfit he knows where he can pull a few strings. Oh, and did I tell you that Phil has put me in touch with friends of his in Highgate, and I can rent cheaply from them - largely because it would appear that their house is being rebuilt around their ears. So with luck I'll have a research job during the day to pay the bills, and I can finish the thesis at night. I just need to kill off the electrifyingly exciting chapter on 'the use of the mask by the nineteenth century essayists', and I'll be home and dry. Then I'll just have to see what fate decides to throw in my way.'

Dave stretched back as far as he could in the forlorn armchair.

'Well we've survived all right on our wits and grey matter so far and there's no reason why that should change,' he pronounced from his recumbent position. 'I look at guys like Phil, knee deep in equations, spending his life in the lab, and with thirty years of equations still to come. His life seems neatly laid out. He's doing something useful and he'll have a good comfortable living, but it all seems so much less clear for us.'

Dave considered his own words for a moment, and then continued, 'But I love what I do and I'm good at it - and my students even seem to be moderately interested. Eventually I'll produce research which will outlast me. The world's a mess, but it'll get worse if we can't provide a decent liberal education. It's the only thing that provides some balance and debate in a world which is moving more and more to extremes. I want to be part of that. I'm ambitious to succeed here.'

Dave drained the last of the tea, and continued. 'But what about you? Where do you see yourself ending up?'

'I thought I wanted an academic future', James replied. 'I really enjoy the research and the college life, but I just feel that if I don't make a break now I'll regret it. I was the first member of my family to go to university. In fact I was the first from my school to go to university rather than borstal! And then making it to Oxford made me feel that I can have a go at anything. Nothing's off-limits Dave. The world's changing, and so are jobs. I mean, what is a business consultant, for example? I've no bloody idea what they do, but I might apply to be one anyway. And jobs in the City hadn't changed for decades, but now some of the firms are employing analysts to analyse whatever it is they do. In fact Haldane has given me some leads there. To answer your question - nowhere specific. I just have an optimistic sense that something will turn up. And in the meantime, I just have to go with the flow, which means tomorrow, and Mr. Haldane.'

'In which case, let's make sure you're suitably fed and watered. Let's pop round to Birching the butcher, get a few rashers of bacon, sausages, bread, eggs, and a bottle of Mateus Rose. Or maybe we've enough for a bottle of le Piat d'Or? We can have a fry up and eat it out here on the savannah.'

Gunn folded his notes, and gathered the tea things. This summer had been the happiest of his time in Oxford. Dave and Phil were great housemates, and his studies were going well. But in truth, he wasn't nearly as optimistic as he'd sounded. His decision to move on to a new life in London was built in part on his own recognition that deep down, he didn't have the dedication and scholarly commitment that he could see in Dave. In that way, Dave had been more helpful than any of the careers people he'd met. And there was nothing for him at home. So he just had to keep moving on.

Back home, his parents were proud of his achievements and that he'd taken advantage of the opportunities they'd lacked. They were retired now, and still living in the grey nondescript housing scheme in the Glasgow satellite town where James had been brought up. His mother, Maggie, had come from farming stock in the north of Scotland and was a proud and resilient woman who carried out her various cleaning jobs with stoic resignation. Maggie never allowed James to see her feelings when her husband left on a tour of duty.

His father, George, had joined the Argylls after leaving school. He'd seen action in Korea, had fought alongside Mad Mitch in Aden, and had undertaken several tours in Northern Ireland, latterly as a sergeant commanding a platoon in Belfast.

For George, education was everything. Education would provide his son with a way out of the hard life he had known, and he pushed James at every opportunity to excel at his school work and to distance himself from the petty criminals and budding gang leaders who made up his classmates.

'You'll hear every excuse as you go through life from those who'll claim to be disadvantaged,' George would say to his son at homework time, 'But you'll never hear them suggest that stupidity and laziness could have anything to do with their lot. The school's where you'll begin to make a life for yourself.'

James had to learn to deal with his father's unrelenting demands, and also to deal with the growing sense of jealousy and resentment amongst his peers, as he began to dominate them academically. They would wait for him outside the school gates and threaten to beat him if he scored more than ninety percent again in the following day's tests. And so the next day, with a mark of seventy-five percent, James would try to explain to his father the kind of pressure he was under in the playground. But George was dismissive. 'You have to ignore these lads or confront them, but you can't let them hold you back.'

The days and weeks passed, James studied and excelled, and became more ostracised. Practical jokes turned into regular bullying, with surreptitious kicks and punches turning into more serious blows as his emboldened classmates grew more confident. It couldn't last.

One morning at break time a group of the most aggressive boys in the class, led by McRae, a particularly venal character who had spent more time in Borstal than in school, cornered James and demanded to see his homework books. James resisted and McRae stepped forward, stood on James's foot, and at the same time head butted him on the bridge of his nose. Blood ran down James's chin and onto his school bag which one of the other boys grabbed and opened, passing the homework book to McRae. James began to pick up his papers and pens and to stuff them back in the bag. As he bent down, McRae held up his book and with a flourish, ripped the pages in two. James had been fearful, and then raging with frustration, but now he felt calm and composed. His fingers closed around the freshly-sharpened pencil in his satchel, his thumb firmly pressed over its blunt end. He rose, and straightening quickly he drove the sharpened point into McRae's right cheek. McRae stood open-mouthed, the pencil point clearly visible, suspended between his teeth. He screamed as blood began to fill his mouth. James turned and walked away as McRae was led off to the school nurse.

It was a gamble which paid off. Of course he was punished and George was called in to a meeting with the headmaster where he assured the school that James would behave with self-control in future. The school was happy for the incident to pass.

They didn't want to lose their star pupil.

But the effect on James's classmates was profound and unexpected. His show of clinical and calculated violence confused their image of him. They developed a sneaking admiration for his quiet self-reliance and they began to leave him alone, and even to treat him with respect. McRae could have remained a problem, but a return to Borstal, this time for a prolonged stay, effectively removed him from their lives. It turned out that McRae's father was at his wits' end trying to deal with his violent son, and rather than press charges, he sought advice from George. As a leader of men, and as a hardened soldier, couldn't he share his thoughts about discipline and control? George was happy to help, but back home his only words to James on the matter were, 'So. Back to ninety-eight percent or better from now on.'

James didn't look back, and in 1975 he was named the Dux of his school and began travelling to Edinburgh University to study law. George and Maggie were thrilled. And James loved this new environment, full of young people who also wanted to learn, and who challenged the very conservative ideas that he'd grown up with. He joined the Politics Society and then the Young Socialists. His head was full of utopian ideas and in his second year he changed courses to study philosophy and English literature.

George had become increasingly frustrated and

ill-tempered each time he returned from duty in Ireland. He and James clashed on almost every subject, and George was deeply disappointed with James's decision to quit the vocational degree. He was frustrated to see the education which he had thought would be the key to a career, begin to fill James's head with concepts and ideas which seemed pointless, or worse, to mock the life he had led. The superficial way in which James and his university friends talked about armed conflict, the threats posed by the Eastern bloc, and the threat of public unrest at home, angered and then saddened him.

At first, James would bring university friends home, but he began to feel uncomfortable introducing them to his modest house and his mother's plain cooking. His friends typically came from more privileged backgrounds, had parents in the professions, and were more familiar with wine with supper, than tea with 'tea'. James hated himself for those feelings, but he wouldn't allow himself to question his friends' motivation. He suppressed the idea that he might be popular partly because he was the token working class friend in the group.

He didn't tell his socialist friends what his father did for a living - that would just be too complicated. He really wanted to feel that he belonged to their world. Their ideas on equality, and wealth redistribution seemed so appealing and so obviously right.

He joined in enthusiastically in discussions about the need to support Callaghan, as the new breed of capitalism which was emerging in the West, threatened to further suppress the voices of socialism in the East. James was impressed by the confidence and sense of certainty which his comrades displayed. Invariably from middle and upper-class families, they stood to lose more than he did by the success of their own doctrine, and this seemed to him to be a mark of their sincerity. He was uncynical. The idea that his friends were indulging in an insincere set of postures didn't cross his mind.

And although James would have quickly denied it, he was also drawn to the group because of the girls who seemed attracted to the ideas of non-conformity and rebellion. He'd had no real girlfriends at school, where he was regarded by the girls as a 'poser' and 'stuck up'. But the girls in the Socialist Society saw James as a good looking guy who was also 'authentic', and they also found him attractive because of his working class roots. He thought they were exotic and fascinating, and he was taken aback at first by their candid attitude to sex. A string of short and intense affairs became the backdrop to his university life.

But then events in Ireland began to deteriorate further. Hardly a day passed without news of another British soldier murdered by a sniper's bullet. Predictably, James's friends were supportive of the Irish Nationalist cause, and as he listened to them fulminate and rail against the illegal actions of the 'occupying forces', he began to feel as detached from them and their values as he had felt detached from the boys in his school.

And then his mother called to say that George had been caught in an ambush in Crossmaglen, and was being transported back to the Royal Infirmary in a couple of days. He had been lucky. He'd been shot in the leg and arm, but was in a stable condition. Three of his men had been killed. The oldest was just twenty-two.

That evening, James attended his final meeting of the Young Socialists. It was a Sunday evening and the members sat slumped in a corner of the student union bar, slowly emerging from their weekend hangovers. The chairman launched into a predictable diatribe on the week's events in Northern Ireland, praising the work of the heroic nationalist freedom fighters in their struggle against the British Army oppressors. After the general chorus of agreement had died down, James rose to speak.

'Actually, this will be my last meeting. I've tried to feel like part of the group, but I just don't see things the same way as you. You're as bigoted as the people you criticise. You're superficial. You're always on the outside looking in. You deal in abstractions, not experience, and you don't want to acknowledge anything like a complex argument, as that would spoil your one dimensional self image.

'My father's in the Argyll and Sutherland Highlanders. He's made several tours in Northern Ireland. Yesterday he was shot and injured, and three of his men, all the same age as us, were killed. I'm proud of my father and I'm proud of what he's done in his career. It's easy to have a principled stance if you're personally unaffected, but you can see that isn't so easy for me. And by the way, I guess none of you've heard the news on the radio. Today the IRA bombed Bristol, Coventry, Liverpool, Manchester and Southampton. It's all getting a bit close to home. But I'm sure your belief in 'the nationalist cause' won't waiver because of that.'

There was an uncomfortable silence. James turned and walked across the beer soaked carpet, the strains of Boney M's Christmas hit beginning to rise from the battered jukebox. He stepped out into the December night feeling good about himself, and looking forward to seeing his family again.

Once he'd got over the shock of seeing his father lying in the hospital bed with wires and tubes attached like some medical spaghetti, James was upbeat, and he succeeded in lifting his parents' spirits, as he had some potentially exciting news for them.

'I know that you disapproved of my decision to drop law and study English, but things are going really well. What if I told you that your son wasn't going to be a lawyer, but was going to Oxford to do a postgraduate degree?'

George and Maggie were delighted and at the same time lost for words. This was something outside of their hopes and experience and the news was difficult for them to compute.

'My professor reckons that I'm on course for a first class degree, and he's encouraged me to apply for a place at St. Gabriel's College. Dad, you've always said I should concentrate on my studies and how right you were. My work is going to have one hundred percent of my time between now and finals. No more wasting time in political discussions and hanging around those wasters in the politics societies. You're going to be proud of me.'

And indeed they were. After graduation day that July, George insisted on taking James to 'The Barras', Glasgow's famous East End street market, where he bought him a second-hand tweed jacket, and an ex hire dinner suit. Its trousers were of an archaic design, with a peaked waistband for button-on braces, and its jacket was faced with fine silk lapels. James thought it was a little old-fashioned, but George insisted that really posh people never throw out clothes, but wear family hand-me-downs until they fall apart. A fashionable new jacket would look conspicuous, but wearing this suit at dinners in Oxford would look like the most natural thing in the world.

George spotted an advert in the Herald. Someone was selling an old cabin trunk, and he insisted on buying it and wrestling it home on the bus. It would look much smarter than the family's plastic Woolworths suitcases, and James would 'look the part' when he arrived at college, dragging it behind him.

Then George decided that he would accompany James on the train journey to Oxford at the start of Michaelmas term. Maggie waved them off at Glasgow Central, making James promise to call once a week, on Sundays. As they rattled through the Borders and sped south, the sense of excitement grew, as much for George as for James. He was delighted that they'd become good mates at the end of the years of painful adolescence.

George stayed at the Mitre Inn on the High Street, just round the corner from James's college. Over the following days they went for long walks around the colleges, punctuated by pints of warm English beer at The Bear, The Kings Arms and The Wheatsheaf. James was intrigued by the way the colleges held a personal meaning for his father. In May of that year the Thatcher government had been elected, and George was a strong supporter of its foreign policy and the changes it was making at home. He also felt a connection with the members of the cabinet. Willie Whitelaw was from Nairn, close to Maggie's childhood home, and had fought in the Scots Guards. For George, Christ Church College meant Lord Hailsham, who had been in the Rifle Brigade. But they spent the longest time visiting New College. This was Secretary of State for Scotland, George Younger's *alma mater*. Younger had been in the Argylls, and had also fought in Korea.

James guessed that his father's perspective on the university was probably unique amongst the other visitors strolling through the ancient college halls and chapels.

George was also impressed that the Rector of St. Gabriel's was Anthony Haldane, renowned diplomat and a cornerstone figure of the Foreign Office for many years before his retirement into academia. 'St. Gabriel is the patron saint of diplomats you know,' George laughed as he boarded the train back to Scotland. 'Who knows where all of this will take you? Before you know it, we'll be seeing you on the nine o'clock news, on the steps of the Foreign Office, sorting out the world's problems with your brain, and not with a gun the way I had to do it.'

'We'll see, Dad. Who knows how things will turn out? Thanks for everything, and take care of yourself and Mum.'

And so James waved him off, and walked past Worcester and the Ashmolean towards his college and his new life.

He found that Oxford suited him very well. While he had found it difficult to fit in at school, and at university in Edinburgh, in the middle common room of St. Gabriel's he found himself surrounded by people who were very much like himself - none of them had fitted in easily in their previous lives. What he and the other postgrads had in common was their academic ability, which in many cases came complete with a large helping of eccentricity. There was very little posturing and self-consciousness, and James found this liberating. For the first time in his life, he forged some strong friendships. Dave was also in the English faculty, Phil was involved in ground-breaking research in the physics department and the others were engaged in a variety of studies across the whole range of university disciplines.

His days followed a regular pattern; up late, lunch in college, four hours in the Bodleian library, drinks and dinner in the college dining hall, then back to the library, before returning to his room in college and working on his thesis until the early hours. He kept fit by running across Christ Church Meadow, and taking karate and judo classes, where he surprised himself by his fast progress.

At first, his only connection with the college hierarchy was with the English tutor who had interviewed him in the Spring, but he soon began to meet the other members of the senior common room at college dinners. It was in Hilary term of his first year that he first met Haldane. He hurried along Turl Street to St. Gabriel's with his gown wrapped tightly around him to keep out the cold and the mist which lay around the colleges at this time of year. Beneath his gown he wore his antique dinner suit, and he felt a mixture of nerves and excitement at the prospect of the evening ahead, as he was to sit alongside the Rector at the top table, a privilege which each of the postgrads took in turn.

Haldane greeted him warmly and quickly put him at ease by recounting his time in Glasgow on government business. They chatted about the city and its landmarks. Haldane was a tall and elegant man. Although now in his late sixties he retained a youthful demeanour, and his carefully combed black hair showed only a hint of grey at the temples. He had an aquiline nose, and extraordinary dark eyes, which held one in their gaze in a way which allowed him to exert control over the direction of the conversation. He orchestrated the table's discussion like an expert conductor, encouraging a shy student to speak here, and challenging an overly-confident speaker there.

The great dining hall fell silent as one of the undergraduates stood to recite the Latin grace. The scene before James was like a Caravaggio. The flickering light from the candelabra which lined each table cast long shadows up into the vaulted ceiling, and onto the portraits of college Rectors who had presided over this scene for over five and a half centuries.

Pringle the butler ordered the first course to be served, and James tucked into the poached fish, enjoying the excellent, perfectly chilled Sancerre which had just been brought up from the cellars. For a moment he struggled to believe that this was really happening to him. He thought of his Mum and Dad now sitting down to enjoy their mid-evening coffee, having finished their 'tea' well before he had even started his pre-dinner sherry.

As the first course was being cleared, Haldane asked Pringle to call for silence, and stood to present his address to the expectant room.

'I'm delighted to be able to welcome you to the Hilary term dinner,' he began, 'and I'm particularly pleased to see the new members of college enjoying the conviviality of the evening and clearly feeling so welcomed and part of college life.

'Your time at St. Gabriel's will be one of the most fruitful and enjoyable of your young lives. College life affords the freedom and opportunity to think, reflect and discuss without the pressures of the commercial world, which of course you'll enter all in good time. Although I don't want to suggest that academia and the world of commerce are somehow separate and unrelated. In fact their relationship makes me think of an incredible incident which occurred at one of our recent Fellows' meetings.'

Haldane turned to half-address professor Porteous, the philosophy don.

'As we were discussing some routine college business, an angel appeared. As you can imagine, we were speechless as she hovered over the senior common room table and came to a halt directly in front of our esteemed philosophy tutor, professor Porteous, to whom she said,

"You are a noble scholar and so I have decided to grant you a wish. I will give you unimaginable wealth or ultimate wisdom. Which do you choose?"

"Wisdom!" Porteous replied, without any hesitation.

'A blinding flash filled the room, and the angel disappeared. We all looked at Porteous, who was now bathed in a golden light. He stroked his beard and knitted his brow in thought. Everything about his person now suggested immense wisdom.

'Finally, I leaned across to him and said, "Say something then, Porteous!"

'Then he mumbled, "I should have picked the money."'

A polite ripple of laughter spread round the room and grew in volume as Haldane basked in the respect and approval of his audience.

'So you see that we don't expect you to study with no practical end result. We know that you'll take your place in society and will have to earn your way, and of course your degrees will help to make all of that a reality. But we do ask you to use the months and years ahead of you in college to choose wisdom. To consider what is important in your lives, and what values you will adhere to, and then to carry those forward with you into your working lives.

'And that brings me, ladies and gentlemen, back to today's world and the evils which are spreading through it as we speak. Our friends in America have asked the UN to insist that the USSR remove its forces from Afghanistan. The Soviets' outrageous invasion of last December is still fresh in our minds, as is the untold suffering of the Afghan people under Russian oppression.

'The Tehran hostage crisis continues with no signs of a resolution, and the Iranians threaten war if America tries to block the straits of Hormuz. Who's to say that Afghanistan is not just a first step, and that the Russians' next move will be on Iran, and on gaining a stranglehold on the West's oil supplies?

'This is the world outside our doors, a world where democracy and civil liberty are threatened daily. Whatever else you learn in your time at St. Gabriel's, you must remember to value our ability to debate openly and the intellectual freedom which we enjoy here: the precious freedom to hear and be heard without censorship.

'Who can criticise the US President for not rushing into the SALT II treaty when the USSR demonstrates such blatant disrespect for its citizens' freedoms? If you're in any doubt about Russia's moral bankruptcy, then consider the fate of the human rights activist, Andrei Sakharov. Arrested in Moscow, and taken to Gorky, a city closed to outsiders. Do you think he'll be enjoying fish and venison this evening? Sadly, I think we all know the answer.'

Haldane sat down to complete silence, as the Fellows and students considered his words. And then, slowly at first, the applause began to circle round the great hall, and then grew louder so that the heavy silver cutlery rattled on the long oak tables.

Haldane signalled to the butler, and the waiters emerged from the kitchens carrying the salvers of venison. He turned to James and poured him a large glass of the Nuits-Saint-Georges which Pringle had placed by his side.

'I hope that wasn't too deadly serious, Gunn', he remarked. 'It's difficult to strike the right balance between levity and seriousness, but these days, the dire state of the world tends to tip me towards the latter.'

'No, I thought that you struck the right chord,' replied James. 'The headlines are incredibly worrying and it feels like any number of the current problems in the Middle East could escalate.'

'So my support for our Western allies didn't upset you, Gunn? I would have thought that with your socialist credentials, you would have been tempted to throw that bottle of delicious Burgundy right over me!'

James was taken aback. This insight into his past was unexpected, regardless of how little the episode now meant to him.

'Don't worry, Gunn,' Haldane continued. 'Just pulling your leg! I know that you haven't darkened the doors of our socialist friends for many months. But I'm intrigued as to why you decided to give all that up. And don't be surprised if I know a lot more about you and your fellow students than I probably should. A lifetime of moving in circles where information and intelligence were the main products has left me with contacts and sources which can prove amusing, and sometimes quite useful.'

James gathered his wits, and explained that he had begun to feel that his left wing student friends were just posturing, that it was probably a healthy phase which they had all been through, but which he now felt was facile and naive.

'So would you say that you have taken sides now, Gunn?' Haldane asked, his eyes fixed steadily on James, who couldn't help but feel a mixture of embarrassment and unease. 'You see, it's very important that we take sides in today's world. Otherwise, we are left in a limbo of amorality where our services can be bought and sold, and we have no right to question or complain. Do you know your own mind, Gunn, or are you drifting along in life? Apolitical, amoral and apathetic?'

'Certainly not, sir,' James retorted, 'Yes, I'm probably apolitical, but I know right from wrong. I condemn the arrest of Sakharov for instance. I'm on the side of what's fair and right and democratic.'

'So would you say you're on the side of your father? How far would you go to uphold those values?'

Again, James was thrown by Haldane's knowledge of his background, and this time he faltered, 'My dad and I didn't used to see eye to eye, but to me he's a hero, and I'm proud of all he's done.'

Haldane flashed a broad smile and refilled

James's glass. 'Of course he is, my dear boy. You can say that to me, with no fear of contradiction or reproach. You can feel at home here. And my door's always open if you wish to discuss any aspects of college life, or just to have a general chat over a glass of wine.'

Before James could respond, Haldane was drawn into the conversation to his left, where a particularly political, moral and apoplectic student was lecturing his neighbours on the finer points of the so-called 'Carter doctrine'. James could almost sense Haldane warming to the challenge of demolishing the outspoken student's arguments. He was about to experience a much less pleasant exchange than that which James had just encountered.

◆ ◆ ◆

And now here he was, twenty months later, preparing for what might be his last visit to the college Rector. Indeed he had taken up Haldane's offer of advice on several occasions, and had grown to like the old boy. Haldane always retained his ability to surprise and throw one off course, but James began to realise that he was also a practical man, and when it came to careers, he spoke with experience, knowledge, and good old-fashioned common sense. He had relatives in the City, and latterly, most of their discussions had been about the possibility of introducing James to their senior partners.

Haldane was a great friend of the foreign secretary, Lord Warrington, and he joked about their time together at Eton. When they were leaving school and discussing their own careers, their housemaster had turned to Warrington and said, "For a really stupid boy, there are three possible professions: farming, soldiering and stockbroking". Haldane cherished this memory and repeated it more than once to James, of course stressing politely that stockbroking had advanced a great deal since those days.

But so far, none of James's letters of application had borne fruit, and for the time being, at least, he was going to fall back on Haldane's 'plan B'; the research job which he had mentioned during the summer.

'Come on James, or Birching will be closed.' Dave's voice boomed out across the garden, breaking the still silence. 'I'm thinking a couple of meat pies as well. Let's go mad!'

'Sure. On my way Dave.' James pushed his way through the straggling grass, balancing the odd assortment of crockery on the stained plastic tray. 'Onwards and upwards to Birching and beyond,' he shouted back, feeling encouraged by Dave's endless optimism to think that tomorrow might just mark the beginning of something good.

# CHAPTER 2 THE AMBASSADORS

James looked at the crumpled tweed jacket which hung on the back of the creaking bedroom chair, and decided against wearing it to the meeting with Haldane. He set the wardrobe door to one side - its hinges had long ago ceased to function - and pulled out his dark grey 'interview suit', the one he had bought in Burton on Oxford Street, and which was identical to that which all of his friends had purchased for their hopeful trips to London.

He stared at his tanned face in the mirror and pushed back his thick fair hair, bleached at the ends from the summer sun. Roman nose, well-sculpted lips and jaw, and deep blue eyes which sat under eyebrows which, like his hair, were thick and unruly. He arranged the collar of the white shirt very carefully, so as to hide the ingrained stains round its neck, and donned the college tie, its light blue stripes standing out against the navy background. Fresh socks and newly polished Oxfords, and he was ready to set out.

It was another hot day, and when he arrived at Haldane's rooms overlooking Chapel Quad, he noticed that all the windows were open. From an upstairs room at the other side of the Quad, he could hear the delicate notes of a Chopin étude as they drifted out into the hazy summer air.

When he reached the top of the staircase outside Haldane's rooms, he could hear the murmur of conversation from within, and then the sound of raised voices. He knocked twice, and stood back. Haldane opened the door with a slightly flushed expression, and ushered him into his spacious study. Pringle the butler was gathering a sheaf of papers and making to leave the room, with a subservient nod to the Rector.

'Thank you, Alexander', Haldane called out to the butler as he closed the door carefully behind him. They listened to his bulky frame and heavy footsteps descending the stairs.

'We can never agree on when we should open some of the claret vintages,' Haldane commented. 'It's a silly thing. Sometimes the debate gets quite heated, would you believe!

'Anyway - very good to see you, Gunn. Come in and take a seat. I'll just go and fetch some chilled Manzanilla which I think you're going to like. And then we can discuss the research role. In fact, we'll do better than that. My old friend, Michael Godfrey, is coming up from town today, and I'm hoping that he'll pop in to give you, and me for that matter, a better idea of the work of the Institute which he's helped to establish.'

As Haldane made his way through to the back room, James settled down on the large red leather chesterfield, and looked around the study. On the heavy oak desk was the photograph of Haldane with Lord Warrington, both thirty years younger and looking confident and commanding. And here also were the photographs of Haldane in the cabinet room, sitting alongside Heath in one, and opposite Wilson in another. A small bronze model of the Foreign and Commonwealth Office building acted as a paperweight on top of a bundle of notes and papers, alongside a long silver paper knife, the handle of which was inlaid with the college crest. On the wood-panelled walls hung a fine copy of Woodville's 'Charge of the Light Brigade', a large and rare Henry Moore print, and somewhat incongruously, a framed poster of a bright and vibrant Kandinsky. Two walls were lined with books in glass-fronted cabinets, ranging in subject matter from classic novels, to biographies of world statesmen, to philosophical works. Again, the collection was eclectic, with works by Milton Friedman sitting uncomfortably alongside those by Keynes and Marx.

Haldane returned, carrying the sherry on a small silver tray, which he set down on the table between the sofa and his high-backed, studded, green leather armchair.

'Looking forward to going up to London?' he asked, 'Have you arranged accommodation?'

'Yes, very much so,' James replied, 'and at first I'll be in digs in North London.' He continued, 'Can I ask, sir, what is Godfrey's role and background?'

'Well *there's* a question which has a fairly complicated answer, but don't let that concern you,' Haldane replied, sipping the rich and cooling drink.

'MG, as I think of him, has been assisting the Foreign Office with project work for as long as I can remember. He's set up a number of invaluable charities and government sponsored organisations in his time, each of which has contributed greatly to our knowledge of foreign affairs and economies. He started out as an academic, and then found himself increasingly in demand by government departments. In that respect his career has been the inverse of my own. Around two years ago, he began to set up an institute which as far as I can gather is engaged in studying international conflict, and also in working with our American allies on the procurement of goods and services.'

As Haldane was about to continue, the telephone on the oak desk rattled a little then produced a tinny ring tone. 'Haldane', he answered. 'Yes. Send him up please.

'But now you'll be able to ask him yourself, James.'

Moments later, Haldane opened the door to a small and somewhat rotund figure, who was clearly struggling with the effort of having climbed two flights of stairs.

'Come in MG. So very good to see you. Allow me to introduce James Gunn, the young man we talked about on the phone. James is seeking gainful employment in London in the financially unrewarding, but potentially intellectually stimulating world of stockbroking. But in the short term he is available to contribute to what is undoubtedly a higher calling - the work of The Soho Institute.'

Michael Godfrey stepped into the room, and fell heavily into the rather tired armchair opposite James. His grey hair was thinning and beads of sweat glistened on his temples. His double chin seemed to squeeze itself over his collar, and the quizzical arc of his eyebrows made him seem permanently uncomfortable and surprised at the same time. His horn-rimmed glasses held lenses the likes of which James had never seen before. They were so thick that Godfrey's eyes seemed to swivel around inside them, adding to the owlish appearance.

He fumbled in a pocket of his waistcoat, which stretched across his body like a large tourniquet. He produced a small silver match box, and swivelling a pipe to his mouth, began unsuccessfully to attempt to light it, flecks of ash spilling meanwhile on the voluminous folds of his trousers.

His voice, when he finally spoke, was quiet and surprisingly soothing.

'Pleased to meet you Gunn, or do you mind if I call you James?' James nodded. 'Good. In fact this is all very good. We need some help doing what is,

I'm afraid, rather dull stuff for a bright chap like you. Sorting facts, keeping reports of events up to date, and occasionally helping our excellent librarian with some lifting and sorting. All very easy I dare say for a scholar of your calibre.'

'That all sounds excellent,' enthused James. 'I'll be finishing off my thesis during my first few months in London. So what you're describing would fit in perfectly with my plans. My thesis is on the Victorian essayists. It's required a lot of careful planning and organisation, so I'll feel very much at home.'

'Goodness! I'm sure that is all very fascinating, James. In fact it looks like everything is going to work out fine,' Godfrey replied a little distractedly. His eyes wandered over the room and alighted on the Kandinsky.

'Oh, Haldane!' Godfrey continued, as if suddenly experiencing a burst of energy. 'Have I mentioned our excellent young librarian to you? You may well know him. He's called Jonathan Clarence. Terribly bright man. Awfully clever. Studied here at Jesus College, and then at the Sorbonne. He is in charge of all our collaborative work with the American Embassy.'

'No. I'm afraid I don't know him, Michael. He sounds impressive. Clarence you say? No, it doesn't ring any bells with me. Will James here be working closely with him?'

'I think you'll be more of a messenger and bag

carrier, if that doesn't sound disrespectful, James. Jonathan has official clearance to see and analyse quite a lot of extremely interesting material, which we should really leave him alone to ponder. As it were....'

Godfrey's voice tailed off once more, and his eyes looped back towards the painting, before studiously attempting to focus once more on his underemployed pipe. James didn't at all mind his description of the role. Being a messenger would be just fine. It was a job, after all, and he was pleased that the meeting was going so well.

'And will I be seeing much of you, Mr. Godfrey?' James asked.

'Very little, I'm afraid,' he replied. 'My work is really in the background. Rather dull subjects like funding and staffing. The Institute's offices are on the edge of Soho, and I won't be far away. I tend to spend more time these days than I should at my club in St. James's. Are you still a member of the Nomads, Anthony?'

'Indeed yes, MG, I am.' Haldane replied. 'Although I rarely visit London these days, and haven't seen the inside of the Nomads Club for far too long.'

Haldane turned to James. 'But you'll continue to see me here at college I trust, James?' You know my door's always open to you, and I would be rather put out if you didn't at least pop in here on your regular jaunts to the faculty offices while you organise the submission of your splendid thesis. Come round and discuss the Victorian essayists with me at any time, my dear boy.'

James sat in silence, surprised by Haldane's show of enthusiasm for his work. He had always been supportive of James, but this degree of encouragement was unexpected. Haldane meanwhile, gazed across the quad, and allowed himself a broad smile. The notes of the Chopin piece still filled the air of the square, and for a moment they sat and listened without speaking. Godfrey had turned his attention to the tightly-packed book cabinets, and seemed to be straining to read the titles on the spines. His fleshy lips were making the shapes of the words as he tried to focus.

Then suddenly he stood abruptly, as if remembering an important engagement.

'Anthony. Must dash. Train to catch. Odd jobs to do first, here and there. So very nice to see you in such fine form, and many thanks for introducing me to James.'

He turned and handed a card to James, which had an address: The Institute for International Research, 19 Silver Street, Soho, and a phone number.

'Call Jonathan on that number tomorrow, and he will sort you out. Dates, pay, rations and that sort of thing. Bye chaps.'

And pocketing his pipe, he struggled to the door, and set off down to the quad below.

James finished his sherry and thanked Haldane profusely for everything. Haldane made him promise to visit on his first trip back to Oxford, and waved goodbye from the leaded windows of his rooms. James loosened his tie and strode back towards Summertown, delighted that he now had a plan, and wondering what thoughts really lay behind those impenetrable glasses of his new boss, MG.

# CHAPTER 3 METRO-LAND AND SOHO

It was a warm Saturday afternoon when James Gunn stepped off the slow train from Oxford and onto the platform at Marylebone, dragging his faithful battered cabin trunk behind him. He glanced at the steps down to the tube, and decided to splash out, and take a cab up to Highgate.

Julia and Simon were to be his new landlords. Phil had met them at Cambridge during his first degree studies, and had been keen to introduce James by phone to this young professional couple, struggling to pay the mortgage on their first home, since marrying after graduating two years earlier. And Steve was to complete the household. Another ex-Cambridge man, Steve was about to start a new job at the Treasury. He would be a good commuting companion, thought James, and someone with whom to explore this new London landscape.

The cab rounded Jack Straws Castle, and then picked up speed as it headed east, along the high ridge which joins Hampstead and Highgate. Looking out to the right, James could see London spread out below him, from the Houses of Parliament in the west, to the shimmering grey and silver towers of the City in the east. The newly-opened NatWest Tower stood tall behind the forest of cranes working on the completion of the new Barbican Centre, and to their right, the serene dome of St. Paul's shone in the early autumn sun.

The cab drew up at 26 South Grove, and James surveyed his new home. The ancient cottage sat between an old coaching inn on one side, and a row of Edwardian houses on the other. Scaffolding covered the front wall, and a tangle of ropes and pulleys hung from a precarious-looking jib arm. A scaffolding tower gave access to the half covered roof timbers where two men stood, smoking and chatting idly. He squeezed between the scaffolding pipes and rang the doorbell.

Julia greeted him warmly. She was dressed simply in combat trousers, a loosely fitting vest and Doc Martens. She ushered him into the sitting room, which was devoid of carpet or wallpaper, but which had been brightened up by large posters promoting CND, and ragged wall-hangings which seemed to James to resemble desiccated sheep.

'Great to meet you James,' Julia enthused, 'Phil has said such lovely things about you, and I think you'll love it here.'

'Really good to meet you too, Julia. The house is great! Really...different. What brought you here? Do you and Simon work locally or in town?'

'Its perfect for our work. Simon's based round

the corner at Hangers the village law firm. He works with socially disadvantaged clients, and occasionally on civil rights cases. I work from home mostly, editing copy for the North London Socialist magazine *The Clarion.* And I'm also helping to set up the Greenham Common Women's Peace Camp. Have you heard about that, James?'

'Oh yes, very much so. Very important gesture. Thoroughly approve,' he replied swiftly.

'And Phil tells us that you'll be doing some very important international relations research?'

'Well, that's kind of him, but I will actually be doing some very dull work. My aim is to finish my thesis and get a job in the City.'

Julia stepped back in surprise. 'Christ! That seems to be a very questionable ambition. I do hope that you're not, how shall I say, 'unsound' politically?'

'Oh, not at all. My aim is to help companies to raise money to... do good things for the environment?' James's voice tailed off in what seemed like half a statement and half question.

'Oh well. It's great to have you in any case James. Your room is upstairs at the back, overlooking the pub kitchens. Not a great view, but some delicious aromas. Sorry about the floorboards. There are quite a few missing at present, but they're on order. They should be here in a couple of weeks. It's amazing how quickly one adapts to stepping from joist to joist. Quite fun really!'

James hauled his trunk upstairs, and set about arranging his things, remembering to avoid inadvertently stepping through the ceiling to the dining room below.

In the evening Julia and Simon bought him dinner at the pub next door, and Steve joined them later. Simon was serious, unsmiling, direct, but perfectly pleasant. He lived for his work, and his passionately-held socialist views. Steve, on the other hand, was from a background more challenging than that of James, and certainly one which was worlds away from those of Julia and Simon. His parents had come to Britain in the early 1950's from Barbados. They had exchanged a small corrugated iron house by the beach near Speightstown for a three bedroom council house in Luton. Despite their courage in travelling four thousand miles across the globe, the West Indian community could be quite reserved. But not Steve's Dad. He had pushed for a job at the Vauxhall car plant, and had grown to become a major voice within the Union. But despite his prominence on the shop floor he had never been formally acknowledged.

With this background, Steve had found that he had to be head and shoulders above his white peers in order to succeed at school, but by sheer force of will and hard work he had fulfilled his ambition to get into Cambridge. Steve was a no-nonsense pragmatist, with an impressive intellect. He knew that he could demolish his friends' arguments easily if he tried, and Simon and Julia maintained a reserved deference when he spoke. Steve thought life was simple. Born with nothing but a very generous helping of brains, he was going to make sure that he made more money than he would be able to spend, and then make a lot more. The Treasury job would lead to private enterprise, investment, corporate engineering and asset stripping. He couldn't wait.

The following day, Steve and James explored their new surroundings. Across a small triangle of lawn from the pub was the house where Coleridge had spent his final years, thanks to the hospitality of the local doctor. James could picture him walking unsteadily from The Grove to the High Street to collect the opium which would hasten his death. And further along The Grove at number seven was the house which Betjeman had described in his poem 'False Security'.

'"I wonder where Julia found that strange, rather common little boy,"' Steve quoted its final lines, and laughed. 'Now our Julia has a couple of common lads to look after as well.

'Seriously though James, that poem still reminds me of the feeling of being an outsider, of not fitting in, of being looked down upon. The snobs at college. The name calling at school, and all the rest. That's what makes me determined to succeed, so that they can read about me and feel fucking stupid.'

'Or they might just carry on in their own

deluded worlds,' suggested James. 'I've come to think that people really just care about themselves. People are selfish. I don't believe in great 'causes' or philosophies. Simon and Julia are lovely people, but who are their efforts for? Aren't they just consumed by middle class guilt, and enslaved by their own political pedantry?'

'Well I know who all my efforts are going to be for. They're going to be for me! And fortunately middle class fucking guilt is something which doesn't affect me. So roll on tomorrow and getting stuck into the job.'

They strolled along The Grove, then turned up to the Gatehouse pub, where they sat outside and downed a couple of beers. The afternoon sun played on the rich red brickwork of the school buildings, and the sword embedded in the cross in the school graveyard glinted through the ornate school gates. Early evening walkers appeared, wandering slowly down the High Street, passing the Prince of Wales and The Angel, and then turning into Waterlow Park. And below the park, in the great cemetery, the giant stone effigy of Karl Marx sternly surveyed the passers-by, silently considering the fruit of his work, which was ripening and falling on distant lands.

Steve and James set off early the next morning. Simon had already left for his office in the village. Julia was practising yoga in the front room as they strode out and walked the few yards to the 214 bus stop.

They hurtled past Parliament Hill Fields, and then the bus ground its way through Kentish Town, before they got off and parted at Mornington Crescent, James jumping on the next 29 bus to Soho. The morning air was bright and fresh but the air upstairs in the bus was fetid and eye-watering from the smoke of at least thirty cigarettes.

James was wearing his only set of work clothes; the tweed jacket, checked shirt, college tie, dark green corduroys and nut-brown brogues. He just hoped that the cigarette smoke would fade from them between bus stop and office.

19 Silver Street turned out to be an ornate Edwardian building set on six floors, with much detailed stonework around the tall windows and doors. Its handsome appearance contrasted with the neglected tenement buildings on either side. To one side was a rather dilapidated shop selling sex toys of which a proctologist would have been proud, and on the other was a traditional butchers shop, selling everything from tripe and offal to sirloin steaks.

James took the old metal-caged lift to the sixth floor, and was greeted at reception by a very large and stern Irish woman, who regarded him with intense suspicion. Her permed hair reminded him of an Italian military helmet, and her large red framed glasses might have been borrowed from Dame Edna Everage. Her impressively-proportioned bosom filled his line of sight. Reluctantly (it seemed to him) she agreed to see if Jonathan Clarence would come and meet him. And even when he had been warmly greeted by Jonathan, and was sitting in his office, she seemed unsure of whether to leave the librarian with this new and unknown addition to the Institute.

'Thank you Mary. That will be all.' Jonathan reassured the still doubtful receptionist, who backed out slowly, but left the door open a couple of inches.

'That was the redoubtable Mary.' Jonathan explained. 'She's the receptionist, security officer, office manager, and self-appointed general organiser of us all. She seems a little intimidating, but actually she leaves me to get on with the important stuff here, and she's very discreet, so it all works out well. She's an old friend of MG, whom I believe you met in Oxford?'

'Yes indeed,' replied James. 'He explained that he has a sort of non-executive role here, and that you run the shop. I'm pleased to be able to help out.'

'That's excellent, James. Its a small outfit, but very friendly, despite your first impressions, and we aim to have fun as well as get through the work. Let me take you out to meet your new colleague.'

James warmed to him immediately. Like James, he was tall and athletically built. Like James, he wore a tweed jacket (but with patches on the elbows) corduroys and brogues. His green tie displayed three stags; the crest of his Oxford college.

His dark hair was parted in the middle and combed flat. Round metal-framed glasses and a neat moustache and beard suggested an academic temperament, but his open charm, and physical presence suggested a man of action rather than a bookish introvert.

'Susan. Meet James. He's going to be with us for a few months to help catalogue overseas news stories and keep the chronologies up to date.'

Sue Almond stood up to shake James's hand, and overturned a pot of pens on her desk, which was piled high with scrapbooks, newspapers and folders. James bent down to help her pick them up.

'God, I'm so clumsy. So good to meet you. Thank goodness I have someone to help me clear this lot. Jonathan has been promising me someone who can read German and French to sort out all these beastly foreign papers. I wasn't expecting...God I'm so bloody clumsy.'

As Sue scrambled to gather her things, a minor avalanche of files slid slowly from her desk to form a small alp of paper around her overflowing waste bin.

'Ah, yes.' Jonathan muttered to James, as Sue crawled under her desk to retrieve the files. 'Foreign languages. I saw on your CV that you're far from fluent in that area James, but to be honest, you're available, and we can afford you. I'm sure you'll pick up the key words and make do. Just wing it with Sue as best you can. See you at lunchtime for a quick sharpener perhaps?'

'Perfect,' replied James to the retreating Jonathan, as he sat down opposite Sue, and began sorting out the desk, which it appeared, they were to share.

James had never met a woman like Sue before. He couldn't make out her shape. Despite the warm autumn weather, above a long woollen skirt she was dressed in what looked like a fisherman's jumper, or perhaps a shepherd's smock. What lay beneath its lumpy folds was a mystery. And her fair hair was stuffed into what looked like a Peruvian woollen hat. Was it long, or short? She seemed oblivious to her appearance. Large brown-rimmed glasses hid the top half of her face. A pretty mouth, devoid of lipstick was the only visible feature which he could discern. Her only piece of jewellery was a small silver charm; a crest with three red stars which hung from a cheap-looking bracelet. Her college crest, thought James. You don't get more square than that.

As James had guessed, Sue was also an Oxford graduate and had been at the Institute for over a year. She had studied music and she loved to talk about her favourite composers. In fact she just liked to talk. She had been starved of company of her own age at the Institute, and now she was going to make up for it by telling James her life story as many times as he could bear to listen. Born in the home counties to a bank manager father and an accountant mother, she'd had a dull childhood, and been to an obscure public school. And then it would appear, a monastic three years at university, where the most exciting events seemed to be a cider-fuelled party or two where she'd passed out before the fun had really started.

But what Sue lacked in terms of interesting reminiscences, she more than made up for in helpful advice about the work. The Institute basically ran on two levels. There was the analysis which Jonathan carried out, pretty much behind closed doors. That was what seemed to interest MG and the other executives who dropped by occasionally. Then there was the gathering of news stories from public sources - generally newspapers and magazines - which were delivered to the Institute in great bundles each day. The work was painstaking and laborious, consisting of cutting and pasting relevant articles and reports into large scrap books which in turn became vast detailed chronologies of events. And the events which they focussed on were any and all reports of terrorist incidents, subversive activities, insurrections and organised crime.

At the end of each week, Jonathan would review their work, and periodically he would send the 'raw material' as he called it, to various consultant writers who identified themes and trends in the data and produced short papers which were then sold to a range of universities and government departments.

Sue explained that she would collate news stories from Europe, and James would collate news stories from the Middle East. They would share the Far East and Africa. Only Jonathan dealt with unpublished material, which came from the American Embassy in Grosvenor Square.

Lunchtime came round quickly, and Jonathan suggested that as his treat he would take the two of them to Daniel's bar at the back of the Café Royal, rather than The Glassblower, which was their usual local. Once inside, Jonathan's eyes swept the wine list and went straight to the top left, ordering the cheapest bottle, which happened to be a Vinho Verde. Sue's sandals looked like large brown pancakes, and between them, her raffia and string bag silently disgorged its contents onto the pristine Café Royal carpet. To the other lunchtime guests it must have looked like two fit young men were entertaining their deranged maiden aunt.

Jonathan had lots of questions for James about college life. Did he know this Fellow, or that student, and how had Eights Week been that summer? Jonathan had been a rowing blue in his final year. And how was James's thesis going? Sue chipped in occasionally, as she seemed genuinely interested in James's studies, and would have been much happier to discuss Ruskin and Arnold than rowing and rugby.

Jonathan turned the conversation to St. Gabriel's.

'I've heard so much about your old Rector, Anthony Haldane. I believe that he's doing some historical research on the Crimean War, now that he's retired from the Civil Service. And that's a subject close to my heart; my undergrad dissertation covered the period, and I still research it as a hobby. I've got some theories about the battle tactics that were employed at Balaclava and Inkerman which I think are fascinating. I'd love to share them with someone who has the same interests. As you can imagine, there aren't many of us around! Will you be seeing Haldane when you go back to have your thesis typed and printed? Maybe you could give him my notes?'

'No problem at all. I have a huge regard for him and he's been very good to me. I've promised to let him know how I'm getting on when I go back.'

James recalled the painting of the Light Brigade in Haldane's study, and vaguely remembered him mentioning some work he was doing on nineteenth century military history.

'Tell me about your work, Jonathan. Is there much you can say?'

'I'd call it a mixture of procurement and logistics. I help Whitehall assess how much overseas aid is required to third-world nations, and I dovetail their ideas with those of the American government. Then there's a bit of a discussion about how to deliver the aid. We're really an outsourced branch of government; they don't have to keep our costs on their payroll, and this way the work's done efficiently and doesn't cost the taxpayer anything. In fact we operate as a registered charity.'

'Oh I see. Christ that's fantastic! It makes sense now!' James replied, enthusiastically. 'To be honest, MG was actually a bit vague, but I didn't want to ask too many questions because I was so desperate - sorry, I mean keen - to get the job. This is great! I'll be able to impress my housemates no end this evening. Wait until they hear that I'm involved in organising foreign aid - albeit not directly.'

'Well actually, we tend not to tell too many people about what we do. People can be so damned nosy. I prefer to just skim over any discussions about work. It certainly makes for a more interesting conversation!' Jonathan chuckled to himself, and then glancing at his watch, he passed a fiver to James for the wine, and took his leave. 'I have a visitor at two o'clock, so mustn't be late back, but you two should stay a while and get to know each other.'

James relaxed into the velvet banquette and poured another glass for Sue.

'Almond.' James pondered. 'Unusual name, Almond.'

'Yes indeed.' Sue replied. 'My Dad used to call up his wayward bank customers and say, "Hello, It's Mr. Almond. As in nut". He used to think that was very amusing.'

They sat in silence for a moment, considering this, then James ventured, 'He's impressive isn't he.

Jonathan I mean. I liked him as soon as I walked into his perfectly organised office.'

'I really like Jonathan,' she said. 'He's like a brother-figure to me. Always very supportive when I feel a bit down. He seems so confident with people. Charming and personable. I'm a bit useless when it comes to new people, or parties or crowds and all that kind of thing. I seem to have changed recently. I wasn't always like this.'

'Hey, come on Sue.' James felt unusually protective towards the frumpy vision sat before him, who had been nothing but helpful and pleasant to him so far. 'Let's not be so gloomy! Do you go out much? Do you have a boyfriend?'

'Yes I do, actually. Julian. He's a musician. He plays violin at the Opera House, so he's out most evenings, and we don't really have much of a social life. In fact he doesn't like to meet new people. He has a terribly delicate constitution and suffers from neuralgia. He doesn't approve of me making a noise, or bringing friends back to the flat.'

James considered the small bubbles in his wine. 'What a barrel of laughs he must be', he thought to himself, but continued to reassure Sue.

'He sounds fascinating, and very...talented.' James was struggling now.

'So what about you?' Sue asked, looking away from James and focussing her thick lenses on the kaleidoscope colours of the bottles behind the bar. 'Do you have a girlfriend? I'm sure someone who is quite - you know - quite good looking like you, must have lots of admirers.'

As soon as the words had left her lips, Sue regretted them. This was not what she had planned. They were to be friendly colleagues, and it was unprofessional to get too personal. She focussed hard on retaining a calm exterior, and began to wish she had left her uncomfortable Peruvian hat at home.

'No one in particular.' James replied. 'There were a few flings back in Edinburgh, and a couple of girls at Oxford who I thought were really special, but they always tended to be with someone else. I seem to make pretty bad choices, but I don't think about it much to be honest.'

Sue regained her composure, and quickly downed the remains of the Portuguese wine. 'Time to head back I think', she said, and began to gather up the contents of her bag and to stuff them back into its voluminous interior. 'That was lovely, James.' she said, as they stepped out into the Soho sunshine.

Back in Silver Street, they were met by an excited Mary, hurrying between the kitchen and Jonathan's office, with trays of tea, then plates of cakes. 'MG has popped in,' she called to Sue as she rushed back to the kettle to make a fresh pot, her military hairdo bobbing back and forth as she crossed and recrossed the rather threadbare carpet of the office.

'He's an odd sort, is MG,' Sue ventured, 'But we owe all of this to him, so I'm always particularly respectful.'

'I only met him briefly in Oxford, and as usual, I thought of plenty of questions afterwards which I could have asked, but didn't. Who funds the Institute, for example?'

'I've had the same thoughts James, and I suppose that the institutions which subscribe to the Institute's reports help with the funding. But I tend not to dig too deep into these things.'

They set about their newspaper cuttings, and soon James had reduced the backlog of work to the point where he felt on top of the collating and chronicling.

MG came out of Jonathan's office and made for the doors to the lift, with Mary fussing behind him. He paused next to James and Sue, and peered abstractedly beyond them, at a small cactus, which sat on the window ledge next to Sue. She called it Cathy the Cactus, which James thought was odd, but very much in character.

'So nice to see you Susan. And welcome to the Institute James. I trust that you are settling in well?'

Relieved by this clear verbal clue as to who Godfrey was actually addressing, James responded enthusiastically.

'And Jonathan is very pleased to have you on board. So that is all very good. Yes. In fact, excellent.'

MG thrust a hand into his waistcoat pocket and produced his matchbox and pipe. He stood for a moment, lost in his own thoughts and contemplating his smoking paraphernalia. After a minute or so, he took a last careful look around the room, and walking slowly towards the lift turned and said,

'Must dash. Odd jobs to do, here and there. So very nice to see you. Bye chaps.' The metal gates closed behind him, and his sparse grey hair descended from sight.

◆ ◆ ◆

That evening in the South Grove household, James enthused to his housemates about his first day. They were impressed by his involvement in organising foreign aid, and Julia beamed at James as she dished up the lentil and bean stew which she had prepared in the makeshift kitchen. Despite Jonathan's mild suggestion that James shouldn't talk about their work, James just couldn't resist the opportunity to impress Julia and to portray himself as someone who fitted into their set of values. He also felt that once pigeon-holed by his house mates, they would probably have fewer questions about the Institute in the future. And this would suit James as he himself had so many unanswered questions about the funding of the place and the workings of the organisation. But he had a job, and some security, and he put those questions to the back of his mind for the present.

The conversation soon turned to politics. Sixteen labour councillors in Islington had joined the SDP, following the defection of the Labour MP Michael O'Halloran. As staunch Labour supporters, Julia and Simon were livid about the move. Steve was also a Labour voter, following his family's tradition and his Dad's union work. He too could see no good coming of this weakening of the Labour Party base, when challenging Thatcherism should be a unifying cause. But he was keen to stress the need to change politics from within, and not to fight the establishment head-on, as his position within the Treasury would have made any more strident argument ring hollow. The discussion carried on long after the remains of the stew had begun to congeal on their plates, until James suggested that they adjourn to the pub, a suggestion which he was relieved to see was warmly welcomed.

And that became the pattern for many evenings to follow, apart from TV nights. Top of the Pops was a regular fixture, and prompted endless arguments about the relative merits of The Police, Queen and David Bowie. And Tuesday nights became a stay-in night to watch a new comedy series about life in Peckham. Julia disapproved of its "patronising portrayal of working class stereotypes", but Simon, Steve and James thought the Trotter family was hilarious.

When the household had turned in for the night, James would work on his thesis for a couple of hours, and he continued to write to firms in the

City, sending his CV in the hope of being invited to an interview. He felt that life was something which was happening to him without him having much control over the direction in which he was going. Perhaps the City would give him the sense of purpose that he was looking for.

But for now he was quite happy to drift along with events. He was in a good place. On that first Monday, the moon rose above the steeple of St. Michael's Church and the bells from Highgate School rang out one o'clock. He wondered what his new colleagues were doing: Sue carefully avoiding disturbing the sleeping Julian, Jonathan grappling with his military theories, MG hailing a cab outside the Nomads Club, his unlit pipe in hand.

His head dropped to the writing table which sat perched on the island of floorboards, and he drifted off into a dreamless sleep.

# CHAPTER 4 A TALE OF TWO CITIES

September passed fairly uneventfully. The seasons began to turn, and the air was cooler as James went for evening walks across Hampstead Heath and around the Highgate Ponds. Soon the old pubs in the Village would be stacking piles of logs indoors, preparing for the long winter nights around their ancient fireplaces.

Life in the Institute was pleasant enough. There was a relaxed and friendly ambience, and even Mary began to smile when James arrived each morning to start another day of reading, cutting, pasting and listening to Sue's latest minor dramas. Her life seemed improbable, her boyfriend sounded insufferable, and at times James was astounded at the banality of her existence outside of the office. But she made him laugh. Her stories bordered on the absurd, and he would swing from being drawn into her bizarre world, to drifting off into his own thoughts. Sometimes he anaesthetised himself mentally during Sue's long expositions, and it was in one of those unguarded moments that he agreed to accompany her to the opera in October. He would meet Julian afterwards, and it would be 'such fun'.

His work on the thesis had taken a leap forward with the completion of the final chapter, and at the end of the month, he arranged to stay in Oxford with Dave and Phil for the weekend, and hand in the manuscript to the typist.

He met Dave in the early evening at The Kings Arms, ordered a couple of pints, and they settled at a corner table overlooking Holywell Street, where students walked and cycled back to town from the English Faculty or were returning to their rooms in Hertford College. Dave was pleased that everything was working out well for James, and found his new housemates and colleagues an endless source of fun and amusement.

'Okay James - so what happened next? No. No. Let me guess - she keeps a journal of his unpredictable bowel movements.' The tears streamed down Dave's face and into his pint of London Pride. 'Did she really have to go into such detail about his lavatorial contortions!'

Now Dave's laughter was bellowing across the pub. James felt a little guilty about repeating some of Sue's more bizarre stories, but he knew that he could trust Dave above anyone else. Dave was the consummate gentleman and was always discreet if he was introduced to one of James's friends.

Dave had news as well. Bridget, his long term girlfriend, was returning to England from her studies abroad and would be living with him in Summertown. They were talking about getting married in a couple of years when Dave had become a more established tutor and had secured a Fellowship. The future was beginning to take a clearer shape for James's friends, and for a moment he felt a little left behind. However, he quickly discarded the thought. Dave and Bridget made a wonderful couple, and he was delighted for them.

'I'm going to buy a bottle of Moët, Dave, and we'll celebrate later, once I've been to St. Gabriel's. I've arranged to see Haldane briefly, and I have some research notes to drop off with him.'

'Then maybe a curry, or we could go to the Chinese Garden for dumplings and crispy duck,' suggested Dave, whose mind rarely drifted too far from gastronomic considerations.

When James arrived at St. Gabriel's, the college was gathering in the cellar bar to enjoy pre-dinner drinks. He hurried round to Chapel Quad and darted up the stairs to Haldane's rooms, where he met Pringle, who was just leaving to organise the serving staff. His usual gruff demeanour had, for once, given way to a friendlier tone, and he smiled and greeted James as he passed.

'James! Dear boy, come in and have a swift one will you?', exclaimed Haldane. 'How about a little Rosebank from the old distillery?' James leaned back in the now familiar chesterfield, and proceeded to describe his work, the characters of the Institute, and his current crop of City job applications. Haldane, in turn, was full of questions. Did he see much of MG? What was the scope of his work, and how was he getting on with the librarian whose virtues Godfrey had so extolled?

James launched into a stream of praise for the Institute's role in organising overseas aid, and for the way Jonathan had made him feel at home.

'In fact Jonathan has done some interesting research into the area you're working on. He asked me if you'd take a look at it, and possibly to give him attribution if you think its good enough. He was a little hesitant about just sending the stuff out of the blue, but I assured him that you'd be more than happy to take a look at it.'

'Of course,' Haldane, replied. 'To be candid James, this paper on the Crimean War started out well, but if I'm honest with myself I've become a bit stuck, and any new perspectives would be welcome. Everyone seems to know about it, and part of me wishes I hadn't been so bold as to say it will be completed by the Spring.'

James was pleased to be able to repay some of Haldane's confidence in him, and placed Jonathan's notebook on the pile of papers, just under the Foreign Office paperweight. They were entitled 'Troop numbers and formations at the Battle of Inkerman'. He stood, and thanking Haldane for his hospitality, sped off to Summertown, stopping *en route* at the off licence.

Haldane finished his whisky, picked up the

small notebook, and flicked through its pages. This certainly looked like interesting analysis. Pringle knocked on the door to say that dinner was about to be served in the hall. 'Indeed Pringle,' Haldane replied quietly, 'Time to get to work.' Pringle nodded, Haldane slipped the notebook into the pocket of his gown, and they descended to the quad below.

James returned to London that Sunday evening, and this became the pattern for a handful of visits over the following weeks. He enjoyed the best of both worlds, exploring London and reuniting regularly with his Oxford friends, while continuing to see Haldane, who seemed to appreciate the stream of notes from Jonathan. He in turn was delighted that his work might well be cited in a paper which would have more exposure than he could ever have achieved on his own.

October arrived, and with it a change of routine. On Mondays, James and Jonathan took a cab from Silver Street to Grosvenor Square, where they would ask the driver to park up at the back of the great, squat Embassy building, from which the giant stars and stripes flew proudly over the west end of the square. They looked like rather odd figures in their shabby tweed jackets and worn corduroys amidst the smartly uniformed guards, who responded to Jonathan's request on the videophone and discreetly let them in to the post room. Once there, Jonathan would have a quiet word with a couple of the guards, and then sign a release document which a smartly-suited member of staff brought into the loading bay. Then they had to carry several bulky boxes of computer printouts back to the waiting cab, and pile them so high that when they were finally ready to set off, they had to peer over the tops of the towers of boxes to see the passing streets of Mayfair.

The process then began in reverse on reaching Silver Street, and by the time James had pushed the last box into the complaining lift, and heaved it into Jonathan's office, the morning was almost over. On these days they didn't see Jonathan again, and would call out their goodbyes to him through his office door.

October also proved to be much busier in terms of news stories to cut and arrange. James usually popped round to La Perla pasta house around mid-morning to pick up Italian coffees and Lisboa pastries for Sue, Mary and himself, and when he returned one Tuesday morning, there was great commotion in the office. Anwar Sadat had been shot while watching a military parade, and the western diplomatic world was responding with anger and outrage. Then the news came through that he had died in hospital, and James set about extracting the various reports of the assassination from the later editions.

As the Middle East monitor, James was also constantly busied with the conflict in Afghanistan, where Ahmad Massoud, the leader of the anti-Soviet Mujahideen was carrying out continuous guerrilla warfare. James filled several books of press reports on the fighting to take control of the Panjshir Valley. He often cast his mind back to Haldane's anti-Soviet speeches. He hadn't expected then to be recalling Haldane's words on an almost daily basis. And then, two days after the Sadat assassination, just when things might have calmed down a little, reports arrived covering Thatcher's whirlwind tour of Pakistan, and her visit to the Afghan border. She had shaken hands with Afghan soldiers, pledged two million pounds of aid to help Afghan refugees, and had vowed to continue to press for the removal of Soviet troops from their land. It was clear that Britain was squarely behind the US effort to rid the Afghan people of the invading forces.

At the end of the busy week James joined his colleagues for a quick drink at the Glassblower. Jonathan had barely left his office all week, and was in particularly fine form, having helped to coordinate with the American Embassy on several shipments of aid, which were due to be transported at the end of November. Sue was also in high spirits. Tomorrow was to be opera day. She had bought two tickets for her and James to see La Traviata. This was going to be a new experience for James, and he had to admit that he was intrigued and looking forward to the evening.

'What time should I meet you and Julian?' he shouted, above the cacophony of the pub.

'Julian?' Sue replied. Her glasses had steamed up, and she was peering at him through the thick cigarette smoke. 'Oh, of course. He'll be getting ready to tune up and do a last rehearsal around six, so why don't we meet at the Marquess of Anglesey around five?'

'Perfect,' James called back, as he backed out through the jostling crowd, and walked along Regent's Street to his bus stop. They were to see the opera from the upper slips, which were the cheapest seats in the house. Sue had explained that they weren't actually seats, but that he shouldn't worry about that, as the magic of the evening would make him forget that he was going to stand for three hours. That was like two back-to-back games at Hampden, he thought, but he was happy to give it a try.

Saturday came, and it was a fine day, so James took the bus to town early, and wandered around Hyde Park corner and along into Knightsbridge. He enjoyed exploring London on his own, taking time to study the buildings and monuments, and looking at the people who were worlds apart from the shoppers he had known in Sauchiehall Street. He sat down for a sandwich in a small cafe opposite Harrods. Condensation streamed down its windows, and made small puddles on the floor next to the formica-topped table where he tucked in to his bacon and egg roll. Suddenly the floor of the cafe shook, and the red and brown plastic sauce bottles bounced in the air and rolled along the floor, spilling their viscous contents as they went. A deafening sound ripped through the room, and for a moment afterwards, James could only hear ringing in his ears. The chef and waiter rushed out into the street to look for clues of what had happened. The streets were full of passers by, each anxiously looking around them, fearful of a second blast.

James made his way east towards Green Park, still shaken by the sound of the explosion, and then walked north into Bond Street. By the time he reached Oxford Street the early edition of the New Standard had appeared on the news stands, and James could see the front page story; 'Chelsea Barracks bombed', along with photographs of the carnage which the nail bomb had caused. This was life in London, where getting off the tube one stop earlier, or randomly deciding to walk north rather than west, might mean injury or even death. He began to see the work of the Institute with fresh eyes. Documenting atrocities like this one, whether at home or abroad, could play a small but useful part in the process of understanding the facts so that others could try to tackle their causes.

He was in a sombre mood when Sue arrived upstairs at the pub in Bow Street. She was wearing her usual multiple layers of garments, and this evening she was sporting a new woollen hat with large treble clefs knitted into the crown. Her wispy fair hair was pushed beneath it, but strands escaped and fell  randomly in uncontrolled bunches onto her high-necked sweater.

'What terrible news, James,' she puffed, as she squeezed into the narrow seat, and looked down at the early evening opera goers below. 'Were you in town? Did you hear it? It makes me so nervous. It could happen anytime, anywhere.'

She was shocked to hear that he had been so close to the explosion, and for a moment he thought he saw a look of deep concern play across her pale features. He found himself cheering her up, and brightening his own mood at the same time.

'Where's Julian?', he asked, remembering that this was to be his first encounter with the delicate violin-playing boyfriend.

'Oh bad news on that front, I'm afraid,' Sue quickly replied. 'He had a migraine coming on this morning and called the orchestra manager to tell him that a replacement was needed. It's such a shame; this would have been a perfect chance for you to meet him.'

James found that he was quite happy not to have to share Sue with the fiddling boyfriend. He found it very easy to be in Sue's company. Once he'd got the drinks in, he could sit back and let her conversation wash over him.

This was his first time at the Royal Opera House and he loved the grandeur of the entrance, the beautifully dressed women, and the thrilling sense of anticipation in the air. He felt that he was a little out of place in his usual outfit of tweeds and brogues, but he was with Sue, who was completely devoid of any style, and they were going to stand 'in the Gods', for three hours, so it was probably both a friendly and fitting look.

They took their places on the bench seats high in the dome of the auditorium, the lights went down, and the delicate notes of the prelude began. James felt an eerie tension building within him, which was broken by the waltzes and the drinking song of the first act. As Violetta moved across stage to sing of her love for Alfredo, James sensed Sue glancing at him in the darkness which enveloped them, but when the lights went up at the end of the first act, she was her usual animated, talkative self.

They had a gin and tonic at both intervals, and James felt very mellow as the third act began to reach its heart-rending conclusion. He was completely entranced by the poignancy of the drama unfolding before him, and his throat was tight with emotion. He moved forward to lean against the slips railing, and Sue followed him. They stood together, shoulder to shoulder, as the final sombre chords sounded.

The lights went up and they both began applauding energetically, nodding their appreciation of the wonderful performance to each other over the din of the ecstatic audience. The vigorous applause went on for several minutes during the many curtain calls.

Once outside they walked briskly down to The Strand where Sue was to catch her bus. It arrived quickly, but they were deep in conversation about the libretto and the history of the opera, and the brilliance of the soprano, and they let two more buses pass before she finally clambered aboard and clumsily waved goodbye, her shapeless handbag almost knocking the hat off the woman sitting in front.

James walked along to Charing Cross, and turned over the events of the day as he boarded the Northern Line train to Highgate. He thought of the opera and how it showed a life cut short by chance, by bad luck. But then he thought about the people killed and injured by the bomb that afternoon. That was not a chance event. It was something which one could at least try to prevent. He thought again about the Institute and the difference between documenting terrorism and tackling its causes. Maybe he should find a career which somehow made that kind of difference. Maybe he was going in the wrong direction with his plans to find work in the City. What did he really want from life, and how was he going to know when he'd found it? Lost in his thoughts, James was only jolted back into the present when he suddenly realised that the train had screeched into the station at Highgate, and the doors were about to close.

As he left the tube and crossed Archway Road,

he thought about Sue, her odd clothes and her odd character. He realised how fond he was of her, in a brotherly sort of way. It was a shame that he didn't feel attracted to her, but somehow that made it easier to be friends.

The last straggling drinkers were leaving the Wrestlers Arms and the Red Lion and Sun as he walked through the Village to South Grove, and he hummed the drinking song from the opera as he headed towards number 26, and bed.

# CHAPTER 5 LUCKY JIM

James and his housemates gathered round the television, and huddled against the cold, waiting for the next episode of Brideshead Revisited to appear on the screen. This was their latest fixed viewing point of the week, and despite Julia's carping about "over-privileged, upper middle class fucking wastrels", they were glued to the set every Monday evening.

The post dinner discussions in South Grove had taken on a familiar pattern. Julia would lambast the government's policies on inflation, decry the level of unemployment, and Simon would carefully illustrate the human cost from the point of view of his clients. Steve would elevate the debate to a general level. Norman Tebbit's comments about his father getting on his bike to find work, rather than going into the streets to riot, had Julia incandescent with rage, whereas Steve saw it as a comment on the need for more social mobility in a changing industrial landscape. James's frequent interventions to suggest that they retire to the Flask Pub usually came just in time to avoid Julia launching the remains of the bean curry at Steve's head.

One thing they all agreed upon was the importance of demonstrating against the escalating arms race. A CND march was scheduled for the 24th, and apart from James, they were all planning to attend. They were disappointed that James would miss it but he had to return to Oxford to prepare for his viva the following week. His degree was nearing completion, and he had promised to see Haldane after the oral exam to let him know how it had gone.

He took the train to Oxford that weekend, and called in at the typist's offices to pick up his copy of his thesis. On Monday he dressed in his interview suit and college tie, and after sharing a hearty breakfast with Dave and Phil he set off from Summertown to attend the exam. He was nervous as he walked briskly past the Sheldonian Theatre towards the faculty rooms where the exam was to take place. His examiner was to be Professor Elwood, the world authority on the nineteenth century English essayists, and someone whom James had revered since first choosing to specialise in that subject. He would have to try to forget that he was sitting in front of his academic hero, and concentrate on Elwood's questions.

It was a chilly morning and there were few people in sight. Lost in his thoughts, James paused to check his watch; the exam was at ten and he had a few minutes to spare. As he looked down, a figure appeared from the cloisters to his left and rushed at him. In a second he had grabbed James's briefcase, which contained his thesis and the notes which Jonathan had given him to pass on to Haldane. James only just managed to cling on to the end of the case, and for a moment, the two men faced each other. James looked down at the shiny nut-brown case, with the letters JG engraved in gold. The briefcase had been a present from his parents when he had secured his place at Edinburgh University. In that moment, James felt as if he were back in the school playground with the threat of savage blows all around him. He quickly sized-up the would-be mugger. He was older than James - probably in his late twenties. He matched James's six feet-plus in height, but he was thicker set and heavier. He was holding the handle of the case in his left hand, and with his right, he formed a large, club-like fist which he drew back, poised to smash into the left side of James's head.

In those seconds James, initially shocked and confused, now felt calm and composed. In one swift movement, he let go of the case, and recalling the moves he'd been taught in karate, swung his body round, and brought his right foot up. The toecap of his well-polished Oxford slammed into the assailant's face, and there was a loud crack as it hit his nose.

His attacker staggered backwards clutching at his face, blood seeping between his fingers. He dropped to his knees on the cold frost-flecked grass, letting out a sharp yelp of pain. The briefcase lay between them, the gold letters glinting in the weak sun. James moved a step forward to pick up the briefcase and his assailant, fearing further punishment, clambered swiftly to his feet and turning, ran towards the High Street, his trainers leaving large footprints on the silvery ground. James picked up his case, checked its contents, and then walked calmly to the faculty rooms.

It was only when he had been welcomed by the porter, shown in to a large and comfortable office suite, and had sunk down into an armchair next to the fire, that he considered the incident which had just occurred. It was if he were waking from a dream in which someone just like him had been the central figure. His actions had been instinctive to the point that he felt that he could disown them. The coldly dispassionate way he had delivered the blow seemed to him like the action of another.

He was lost in this train of thought when Elwood appeared in the doorway along with a senior member of the English Faculty. And once they had made their cordial introductions they sat opposite James and the discussion began, putting all thoughts of the earlier incident out of James's mind.

Two hours later James stood at the bar in St. Gabriel's, relishing the first long draught of the amber beer which Dave had set up on the ancient brass-topped counter.

'Congratulations Jamie,' he boomed, his voice

rising above those of the pre-lunch drinkers and echoing off the low cellar ceiling. Dave, Phil, his closest friends from the English Faculty, and a few undergraduate girls had gathered to drink a toast to 'James Gunn, newly crowned Master of Letters.'

The examination had gone so well that James had hardly noticed the time passing. Elwood had seemed genuinely interested in his thesis. They had spent at least half an hour dwelling on the later writers like Wilde. They had debated Wilde's use of masks to both express the truth, and also to disguise it. Their conversation had strayed to Macbeth and his claim that 'nothing is but what is not'. At one point, he thought that Elwood was trying to tease him to say something which was just out of James's grasp. Perhaps a point about the subjectivity of his analysis, or even a point about the subjectivity of our own understanding of the world around us? Was everything as it seemed? James responded, finishing the discussion with an acknowledgement of the many interpretations of the works. But he also presented a robust defence of his own interpretation.

At the end of the viva, Elwood stood up, and shaking James's hand, thanked him for a most engrossing debate, and said that he had the greatest pleasure in recommending him for the title of Master of Letters. He'd decided that he was worthy of the degree from the moment he'd picked up his thesis, and the viva itself had simply been a pleasure that he'd been looking forward to.

James was overwhelmed, and shaking Elwood's hand with great enthusiasm, he made his way to the phone box on the High Street just outside University College.

'Mum, Dad,' he called into the phone, when George had answered. 'I did it it! The viva went really well. I'm going to be an M.Litt.'

George and Maggie called their congratulations down the phone. 'Does this mean that you'll get a pay rise at the Institute?' George asked, his excitement brimming over. 'Will you get a bit more in the pay packet?'

'I'm afraid it's not like that, Dad,' James replied, 'but it'll really help me in my job applications in the City. Remember the Institute's just a stop gap. I'm just there to tide me over while I try to get a proper job.'

'But you know a job's a job, Jamie,' George replied. 'I don't understand why you don't just make the most of what you've got. Why do you have to keep making changes?'

'Look Dad,' James replied, 'It's a different world down here. Don't worry about me. I'll end up in the right place. It's just that I don't know what that place is yet. Don't worry. Look. I've just landed a Masters degree, for goodness sake. Let's just enjoy the moment!'

'Well I don't know, James.' George replied, 'but I'm sure you're right. Have a great time this evening. We're proud of you and we're behind you. Whatever you choose to do…' His words began to falter and his voice tailed off.

James was silent for a moment. It was unlike his father to show even this small degree of emotion. This was very unfamiliar territory. There had been the occasional hug from his parents, when setting off for university, but in general, shows of emotion were rationed to the rare moments at New Year, when the whisky and the atmosphere penetrated the usual formal boundaries.

'Thanks Dad,' was his lame response. 'I couldn't have done it without your support.'

After a silence that seemed to last for minutes, George responded in an unusually hearty manner, 'We're going to send a cheque in the post tomorrow. Have a few drinks on us, son, and enjoy yourself for a few days.'

'That's fantastic, Dad.' James replied, relieved that the conversation had reverted to the usual comfortable level.

And now here he was at the bar in college, knocking back his second pint, allowing the effect of the beer and the unwinding of the exam nerves to wash over him. It looked like the party was set to continue into the afternoon and evening. 'Give me half an hour, Dave,' he called across the bar, 'I said I'd visit Haldane, and I'd better pop round to Chapel Quad now, before I start slurring my speech.'

'We'll set them up, Jamie. See you in half an hour

and don't be late,' Dave shouted back, through a mouthful of chicken and mushroom pie.

He found Haldane in a distracted mood. Pringle and he were just finishing off some college accounts, and he asked James to take a seat on the old chesterfield while he signed off some kitchen orders. Pringle looked his usual prickly self, but his mood seemed to lighten on James's appearance.

'Good to see you back, Mr. Gunn,' he muttered as he gathered his papers and made his exit.

'So. What news James?', Haldane exclaimed, relieved that the dour Pringle had taken his leave. 'How did it go with Elwood? He hinted to me last week that he'd found the thesis most impressive.'

'It went extremely well, Mr. Haldane,' James responded, 'I am now a Master of Letters, and I couldn't be happier.'

'This calls for a glass of something special. Pol Roger, I think. Let's enjoy a glass of Churchill's favourite plonk! I have a couple of bottles squirrelled away in the back room.'

Haldane left to fetch the bottle and glasses, and James surveyed his desk, which was less tidy than usual. Sticking out from under the piles of notes for his Crimean paper were maps and diagrams, with what looked like inventories and various lists. But James's attention was mostly taken up by the new telephone on the corner of the desk, which had replaced the old tinny handset. It had a recall feature, a system for storing numbers, and a rudimentary speaker which could allow hands-free conversation. It was also compatible with the new phone sockets which were soon to be introduced. James was impressed.

'Quite a machine, isn't it?' Haldane saw James's gaze as he came back holding the chilled champagne in one hand and two glasses in the other. He placed them on the desk, and noticing the untidy pile of documents, quickly marshalled them together, and placed them neatly below the familiar Foreign Office paperweight. 'It's a sign of progress. Not standing still. There will come a time when even sophisticated machines like this one will seem old-fashioned. I've seen designs for telephones which one can actually carry around with one. Quite extraordinary. At present they would just about fill your briefcase, James. You may think my ideas fanciful but I can imagine smaller versions, which might actually have a wide appeal. Can you imagine everyone walking around with a little personal telephone apparatus?' Haldane paused, realising that his flight of fancy was a little out of character, and settled down in his armchair.

They savoured the first biscuity taste of the chilled champagne and discussed James's recent work at the Institute. Haldane had very strong views about Thatcher's recent visit to the Afghan front line. He was passionately in favour of the gesture. He was in part influenced by his old friend the Foreign Secretary's trip to Moscow that summer to attempt to broker a means of Soviet withdrawal. Haldane's anti-Soviet instincts had been hardened by the involvement of his old school chum. Lord Warrington had returned with an optimistic message that the proposals had not been turned down, but for the Russians, Andrei Gromyko declared that the plan had no future.

They turned to Haldane's work on the Crimean war which was beginning to take much better shape.

'That reminds me,' James said, digging into his briefcase, and placing a small notebook beside the phone. 'Jonathan at the Institute has some additional notes on the battle of Balaclava which he asked me to hand to you. Can I ask if you'll mention him in the footnotes?'

'Tell him I'll go one better than that. I'll mention him up front in the acknowledgements. It's the least I can do for his helpful insights.'

'He'll be delighted with that, sir,' James replied. He would call Jonathan with the news a little later and tell him that he would spend the night in Oxford take the first train back to London in the morning, and be at the Institute around ten.

'I do hope that we'll continue to see something of you in future,' Haldane remarked, holding the crystal champagne flute up to the October sunlight which was threading its way through the leaded windows of the study.

'You're an excellent example of diligence and

hard work, and of the success which that can bring. I would like you to attend the odd college dinner, and share your experiences with the undergrads. And of course, if you do happen to land a job in the Square Mile, then that too would be worthy of discussing with our younger students. I can see the way that Thatcher is shifting the financial world towards deregulation. There's even talk of doing away with dual capacity, which would let American banks, and their money, into the British system. It seems far-fetched today but City salaries might even become quite attractive.'

'A job in the City's still my main hope, and now the thesis is complete I can devote myself to pursuing that goal.'

He felt lucky that Haldane had picked him out of the crowd because of his character and attitude, and that he had thought of him for the Institute role.

'I should really go now. A few friends are buying me a couple of drinks, and I don't want to keep them.'

'Of course James. I'm delighted that you dropped by. Oh, and thank Jonathan for his notes. One day I'll actually get to meet the chap. He sounds like a thoroughly decent man. Give him my thanks, and say hello to MG when next you see him.'

James returned to the college bar where yet another round of drinks had been set up, and the noise level was now quite deafening. He went off briefly to call Jonathan, who was delighted with his news, and then returned to attack another pint of ale.

'Stick some money in the kitty, Jamie,' Dave's voice resounded round the cellar walls. 'You know the form. Drunk for a fiver, dead drunk for a tenner. Dead for fifteen quid.'

A drinking game ensued which James knew was bound to end messily. Several beers and a couple of kümmels later, he emerged with the rest of the drinking crowd, blinking in the late afternoon sunlight. They headed for Browns restaurant where at least, James thought, he would be able to soak up some of the alcohol with one of their famous Guinness pies.

More drinks followed at the restaurant - this time several bottles of claret - and he began to feel the room swimming around him. Conversation seemed effortless, the words of his friends seemed quite brilliant, and he was oblivious to the noisy gibberish which was, in reality, rising ever more loudly from their table. He couldn't recall exactly when the history undergrad with the glossy black tights, clinging black dress, and soft red lips appeared next to him, but as the evening progressed, and the room around him became blurred, he found that they were kissing with such vigour that Dave threatened to douse their very public passion with a nearby fire extinguisher. It was at this point that the manager suggested very politely that they settle the bill, happily agreeing to supply half a dozen bottles of wine and some beers so that they could continue their celebrations elsewhere.

Back at the house in Summertown, Phil put Queen and Bowie's just-released single on the turntable, and the crowd of around a dozen friends and new acquaintances began to dance to *Under Pressure*. Dave began to organise a monster fry-up, the dancing continued, and James, who at this point was seeing the world through a pleasant fog thought it prudent to retreat to the spare bedroom. A small voice somewhere in the deepest recesses of his still-functioning brain reminded him of the early train which would be waiting for him the next morning. The room was in darkness, and he quickly threw off the interview clothes. He slipped, naked, between the cool sheets, not noticing the black dress and tights discarded on the bedroom floor.

# CHAPTER 6 THINGS FALL APART

James was woken early from a deep sleep by the screeching of cats rummaging amongst the dustbins below the bedroom window. His head ached, and a drowsy numbness filled his senses. The history student, it transpired, was called Polly. One of the most assertive people he had ever encountered, she knew exactly what she wanted. Sex. And a whole lot of it. James had barely had a couple of hours sleep. He gazed at her as she slept, and thought how very beautiful and peaceful she looked. They had talked into the early hours of the morning, and James had been impressed by her self assurance, and the confident way she seemed to know what she wanted from life. She got what she wanted. But more importantly, she knew what that was. By contrast, he felt unsure and confused.

Her arm lay across his chest, and he carefully moved it before attempting to sit. He felt wretched as he stood up, and the room began to swim around him again in an ugly version of the previous evening. He dressed quietly, pulling on his tweed uniform and packing his suit in a holdall. His mouth was dry, and he thought he might retch at any moment. Polly was stirring as he was about to leave.

'See you again maybe, James,' she whispered, pushing her thick black hair out of her mascara-smudged face, and trying hard to focus.

'Sure.' he replied, kissing her softly. 'Last night was amazing. I'll look you up next time I'm around college.'

He picked his way carefully through the party debris. Empty wine bottles littered the floor, and in the corner of the sitting room, the record player continued to spin Queen's Greatest Hits. Thankfully someone had had the presence of mind to set the stylus on its cradle. He switched off the turntable, and squeezed past a fully clothed Phil, who lay prone on the battered sofa, and walked out and along to the Woodstock Road.

It was early, and he would have no trouble catching a London train to get him to Soho on time, so he decided to pass the bus stop and walk to the station to try to clear his head. But every few hundred yards, he felt so sick that he had to stop and take lungfuls of air.

He bought a bacon roll at the station kiosk and a paper cup of weak coffee. Once on board, he stared at his unappetising breakfast, unable to summon the courage to let anything pass his lips. His head was now beginning to throb, and his insides were churning like a booze-filled washing machine. He held his briefcase tightly on his lap to stop his hands shaking. He felt a mixture of self-pity and self-loathing. Flashbacks from the evening swept back into his mind, and fragmented images of the restaurant, the bar, and the energetic Polly raced around his brain. He stared out at the passing London suburbs, in the hope that his mind would focus by the time he arrived at Marylebone.

The station clock showed 9 am as he stepped off the train and walked slowly and deliberately across the concourse towards the tube. Four stops, ten minutes. That was all he had to endure in this rattling underground hell, made worse by the packed carriages and his realisation, too late, that he had boarded a smoking compartment. Half burning cigarette ends were stuck between the wooden grooves on the floor, and his stomach began to perform somersaults once again.

Piccadilly Circus seemed like heaven by contrast, despite the choking fumes from the buses and cabs. He walked past the Café Royal, and into Brewer Street, stopping at La Perla to pick up the morning coffees. He slung his holdall over his back, and walked along to Silver Street, balancing three cups of cappuccino on a tray in one hand, and a bag of Lisboas and his briefcase in the other.

At number 19 he squeezed into the lift and managed to close the concertina cage door with his elbow. He leaned his head back against the mirrored panel of the lift and closed his eyes. At last he was beginning to feel almost normal. He thought again about last night, and surprised himself by feeling a pang of guilt about Polly. How was he going to describe the evening to Sue? He would apply a heavy edit to its later stages. Then he began to feel exasperated with himself; why did he care what Sue thought? He would tell the whole story, but minus the intimate details.

He struggled out of the lift, and paused at reception. No Mary, which was very odd at this time of the day. He peered over her desk, and everything seemed neatly organised as usual. The door to his office was slightly open, which was handy, given that he was still balancing the coffees, and he pushed it open with his shoulder and entered.

He scanned the room quickly and his heart missed a beat. He stood motionless, transfixed by the scene before him. Mary lay on her back in the middle of the office. Her tweed suit was impeccable as usual, the long skirt smoothed down over her sturdy legs. And her heavy brown leather shoes pointed up at the ceiling. But her head! Her helmet of hair was now shattered and matted. Her red-framed glasses were smeared with blood. Her head was tilted a little towards him, and he could see that blood had run from her mouth, and had formed a large congealing pool beneath her head.

James was in that confusing state of shock where the mind cannot make sense of what the eyes can see; and in his confusion, he wondered why he hadn't noticed Mary's sensible shoes before now.

Over to the left of the room in front of the window his desk had been overturned, and papers and files lay strewn across the old carpet. At first he thought the space behind the desk was empty, but then he saw Cathy the Cactus lying forlornly on her side. He stepped forward, looking over the desk. The coffees and cakes fell from his hands, coffee splashing his brogues as he recoiled at the sight of the figure which lay hunched amidst a blanket of newspapers and notes. He couldn't see her face but he could see the top of Sue's woolly hat. It was slightly flattened on one side; a wide black mark looked like it was still slightly smouldering. Dark red blood had seeped out of the wound and had soaked her hat, so that its weight made it sag heavily down to her neck.

James thought he was going to be sick, and he doubled over clutching his briefcase, his holdall sliding up and hitting him on the back of the head. Then out of the corner of his eye to the right, he caught a glimpse of Jonathan's head, just protruding from his office, the door of which was slightly ajar. He lay facing away from James, his head and shoulders one red streak of blood. His collar had been pulled back, and James could see a dark red line around his neck, as if he had been strangled before being shot.

James's hangover had vanished, and now his mind swam with terror and confusion. Then suddenly, the whispered tones of what sounded like Arabic voices from inside Jonathan's office jolted him into the present.

James froze. He heard a rustling of papers and then the click of a magazine being locked in place, and then more whispered voices.

They had heard him. Footsteps began to cross Jonathan's study, and then came a loud shout as James half ran, half staggered back to the lift. He threw himself against the glass panel, smashed the iron gate shut and stabbed repeatedly at the ground floor button. The lift began its descent, and as the top of his head dipped out of sight, James could see two men run to the lift, frantically pushing the call button. They wore balaclavas, black jackets and combats; one carried a handgun, the other a short rifle with a silencer. He swung his briefcase up to obscure his face as he heard them begin to descend the stone staircase. He didn't think they'd seen him, but he could take no chances. He would turn left, quickly turn left again, and run the length of Brewer Street, hoping that the mid-morning crowds would afford some cover. Then at Wardour Street he would turn neither left nor right, but dog-leg into Old Compton Street and keep running.

As he ran east the sweat from his hangover and his exertions began to drip down the small of his back. He glanced round briefly and saw the two men running along the middle of the road, checking the side streets as they went. Their balaclavas had gone, revealing short hair and beards, but he could make out no features given the distance between them.

At the junction with Wardour Street, he did a mental check on the contents of his holdall. There was nothing in there which could give away his identity, just the Burton suit, an old shirt and yesterday's underwear. They were welcome to it all if they wished and it might distract them for a moment, so he dropped it in a waste bin as he sped past The Admiral Duncan. His shirt was now sticking to his back and his legs began to tire. As he approached Frith Street he made a lurch to the left, apologising as his briefcase almost toppled a cyclist, and darted into Bar Italia. He walked briskly to the back of the narrow bar, breathing slowly to try to regain his composure. He ordered an espresso, and stood between two burly street cleaners who were enjoying a quick break. He peered round them at the street outside, his heart still thumping in his chest.

After a few minutes he saw the two men in black. They both carried cloth bags, presumably holding their firearms, and one of them had James's holdall. They walked north towards Ronnie Scotts, glancing into the bars and restaurants to either side of the street. They vanished from view for a moment and then he saw them run at speed back towards Old Compton Street.

He ordered another coffee and tried to organise

his thoughts. Had anyone survived the attack? Perhaps he should he go back to the Institute to check. But what if the building was being watched? What if there were more of these people? How would he even identify them?

He couldn't shake off the image of Sue's crumpled body. He began to tremble with a mixture of fear and shock, and clung to the bar to steady himself. Who would want to do this? Sue was harmless. Jonathan's hobby was studying nineteenth century battlefields, for God's sake. And Mary was the epitome of a homely maiden aunt. This was obviously a case of mistaken identities. A huge and terrible mistake.

Who were the assassins? The Arab voices must offer a clue, but the Middle East featured no more than any other region in his and Sue's work. And how could they be relevant to Jonathan's foreign aid work? It made no sense.

He thought again; was there any chance that they might survive? He had to call the police and ambulance. Yes; that was the obvious thing to do.

He walked to the back of the cafe, picked up the phone, and dialled 999. His call was answered quickly, and he requested the emergency services, gave the address, said that there had been an attack, and urged the operator to get someone on the scene as quickly as possible.

'Can I have your name please?'

James hesitated. Would he be a suspect? What

had he walked in to? He couldn't think straight. He hung up the receiver and walked back to the bar.

He tried to gather his thoughts. What was he going to do now? He needed time to form a plan. Firstly, he had to make sure that he was safe, and wasn't being followed. If he ran north, and away from the two men, he could take a right at The Dog and Duck, slip through to Greek Street, then along the narrow alley which led to Charing Cross Road and the Northern Line.

He saw no suspicious characters along the route, but when he arrived at the bustling tube station, he felt cornered and on the edge of panic. Down in the dusty white-tiled tunnels there was nowhere to run or hide. A Northern Line train rattled towards him heading north, but at the last minute, he ducked down the connecting tunnel and took a south-bound train to Charing Cross. There he reversed the process, and once settled on the northbound train to Edgware he began to gather his thoughts. The carriage was almost empty, and the other passengers seemed to be buried in their newspapers. After another change at Camden onto the Highgate branch he began to relax.

It was a cold, crisp sunny day as he walked up to the village. Winter was on its way and the trees around the station were looking bare and dejected, their trunks bearing the grey dust from the endless thundering traffic on the Archway Road.

It was lunchtime and the boys from Highgate

School filled the narrow lanes round the High Street, shoving and pushing in a display of unleashed energy. This picture of normal village life was reassuring, and James wanted to grasp it with both hands as a counter to the images which continued to flood back into his mind.

He stood in the sea of blue blazers in Brockley the newsagent, patiently waiting for the boys to buy crisps and lemonade, and flicked through the early edition of The New Standard as he queued. There was nothing about the incident on the front page, just a story about the resignation of the Finnish President, and more pictures of the huge CND rally at the weekend. He bought a sausage roll, some drinks, a sandwich and the paper, then chose a quiet corner of Pond Square to study it in detail. There was nothing there. How could a triple murder not even make the inside pages? He would have to be patient and check the later edition. But then he thought - what if this was a bigger story which the authorities wanted to keep to themselves, and deal with out of the public gaze? He started searching his memory again for clues. Had Jonathan said anything about deals with the Middle East? Could it have some connection to the work he was doing with their friends in Grosvenor Square? However he tried to make sense of it, he quickly ran out of ideas and inspiration.

He began to walk across the square towards number 26, but as he neared the junction with

Bacon's Lane he froze with fear, and darted behind the wall of The Old Hall. He had spotted three men lingering outside number 26, two at the front gates to The Hall, and the other by the entrance. He couldn't be sure, but he thought that two of them looked a little like the men who had chased him. Or maybe they were just part of the larger group of workmen who were still putting the finishing touches to the roof, and who clambered along the scaffolding, or paced back and forth to their nearby van.

Bacon's Lane was a cul-de-sac, but there was no way that James could go back to South Grove without the risk of being spotted. So he walked to the last house in the row. There was no car in the drive, and no movement through the windows of the lounge. So he darted down the side of the house, crossed the garden, and then clambered over the wall which led to a steep drop to the graveyard below. Landing on top of his long-suffering briefcase amidst a giant mound of leaves and mud, he picked himself up, extracted the assorted foliage from his hair and clothes, and made his way to the Circle of Lebanon - the sunken circle of tombs which sits in the shadow of St. Michael's Church, where he would be able to hide safely.

He couldn't go back to South Grove and he was reluctant to risk another tube journey. He had enough food and drink to last until tomorrow, and he considered his options. He decided to wait until it was dark and then look at everything with a fresh mind.

He wedged himself into the entrance to one of the tombs, drawing his knees up to his chin to keep out the cold. The vault held the remains of the poet, Radclyffe Hall, and on the left of the entrance there was an inscription which read;

"And, if God choose, I shall love thee better after Death."

James recognised the lines by Elizabeth Barrett Browning. He thought of Sue, viciously gunned down for no reason. He already missed her daft stories, and even her eccentric appearance. She was pretty much the only girl that he could talk easily with, and now she was gone.

The sweat had dried on his clothes, and the tomb was dry and sheltered. He suddenly felt exhausted, and using his briefcase as a pillow, he curled up and slept the sleep of the dead.

◆ ◆ ◆

He awoke with a start to the sound of crows the size of small dogs clattering their wings in the corridor between the tombs. They had spotted his half-eaten sandwich in the fading light of dusk, and were making ever-bolder forays towards it. He sat up and threw the food towards the entrance to the burial chambers, and the crows followed, their rasping calls shredding the stillness of the early evening.

It was almost dark and James stood quickly, stamping his feet to get the circulation and warmth back into his legs as the events of the morning flooded back into his mind. He had to speak to someone to try to make sense of it all, and the person he could most trust to give sound advice was his father. He would find a phone somewhere discreet, and he would call George.

He walked purposefully down the Egyptian Avenue towards the cemetery chapel and gates. The spectral shapes of ivy-clad urns, and the curve of stone angels' wings lined his path. He was relieved to pull the great gates behind him and set off down Swains Lane.

He turned left at the bottom and walked between the high Victorian terraces towards the Star Pub, whose brightly-lit interior shone like a beacon in the darkening street. The pub was bustling with early evening drinkers and he had to squeeze past the locals to reach the bar. He felt safe in the midst of this crowd, and the ordinariness of the scene. He ordered a pint of Guinness and took it over to stand by the open fire where the heat, the velvety stout and the fragrant wood smoke restored his sense of calm, and cleared his mind. He picked up a discarded copy of the late edition from a nearby table and scoured its pages for mention of the incident, but again there was nothing.

The pay phone hung on a wall in a quiet passageway to the kitchens, so he was unlikely to be overheard. He searched his pockets for change, and then picked up the handset and dialled.

'James!' His father called on hearing his voice, 'To what do we owe this pleasure? It's not a Sunday is it? Is there something wrong?'

'Dad, it's difficult to know where to begin. I'm fine. Don't worry about me, but something has happened and I need your advice.'

'Aye sure. Go on.' George replied, both relieved and wary.

'I can hardly believe I'm saying this, but I went into the Institute late this morning and,' he paused, finding it difficult to form the words, 'my colleagues were dead. They'd been murdered.'

After a short pause, George replied slowly, 'I don't understand. It's a library, an office. What happened?'

'They'd been shot. I think I saw the gunmen. Two guys chased me but I escaped.'

'Where are you now? Are you safe? Have you told the police?'

'I'm safe. I got away, and I'm being really careful. I called 999 but then I just got away from the scene. There's something odd about all of this. It wasn't in the paper. I think they must have been terrorists. I don't know who I should trust.'

George thought for a moment. What had James got himself caught up in? George's job was the one where you got shot at. James was just a student. An office worker.

'James. Who do you think would be best placed to help you? Someone you could have some confidence in?'

'I guess it would be Michael Godfrey,' James replied, 'But apart from his club, which is dangerously close to the Institute, I don't know how to reach him. I suppose that if I could get to Oxford and speak to Anthony Haldane, he'd be able to speak to MG and clear this up. Then once I know what's going on, I'll go to the police and see if I can help them, if Godfrey thinks that's appropriate.'

George turned this over in his mind. It seemed like a good plan. James didn't know if he was still being followed, but if he could catch an early train to Oxford, rather than stay in London, it might be safer, and hopefully Haldane could make the right enquiries.

'I think that sounds like a good plan, James. I can't really advise you, but as long as you can stay safe, then that's all that matters. Where will you stay tonight? Are your digs safe?'

'I don't really know, but don't worry. I'll find somewhere to stay. Look, I'd better go now. Speak to you tomorrow. I'll call from Oxford once I've had some advice from Haldane. Don't worry Mum with all of this, please. By tomorrow, everything will be fine.'

James threaded his way back to the bar, feeling better for having shared the awful story. He ordered another pint, hoping that it might provide the inspiration to help him figure out how to spend the night safely, and be close to Marylebone for an early start in the morning. And inspiration did come - literally - from the glass of black liquid. Guinness. Not Arthur, but Edward, who had bought Kenwood House in the 1920's. This splendid Adam mansion stood in parkland to the north of the Heath, quite close to The Star. He remembered seeing an old derelict dairy to the west of the great house. This was the answer. He would stay there tonight, and then walk down through Belsize Park and St. John's Wood in the morning.

As he left the pub he spotted a couple of blankets lying on a wooden bench for drinkers braving the evening air. He scooped them up as he made his way towards the Highgate Ponds, and up the steep slope of Parliament Hill. The Heath was deserted and he felt confident that he was making the right decision. At the summit, he paused to look across London which lay before him like a vast black sea, a million lights floating upon its surface. To the east, St. Paul's dome sat reassuringly on the horizon, and to the west, the lights of Westminster Palace sparkled through the cold night air. A soft and constant reverberation rose up from the metropolis, and the occasional sound of a car horn or a train rattling its way from Kentish Town to Hampstead broke the silence of the Heath.

He turned north towards Kenwood, and was

soon passing the grand stucco-fronted building, its white walls rising in ghostly columns against the darkness of the sky. He walked on, and when he reached the old dairy, he found that the door was loose on its hinges, just as he remembered. It took no effort to push it open, and once inside he used a lighter from the pub to find a sheltered corner which was dry and clean. He settled down under the pub blankets, and rested his head against his briefcase. From this position, he could see across the fields to the south, and he knew that there were no entrances from the north. There were exits right and left, and he guessed that he would hear footsteps if anyone approached. He felt secure. And so it was in the role of hunted but defiant prey that he eventually drifted off. But his sleep was troubled by bloody figures which forced their way into his dreams, and laughed cruelly at his helpless ignorance.

# CHAPTER 7 DECEPTION

He found it difficult to believe that it was only twenty-four hours since he had been on this same train, wrestling with his hangover and looking forward to an uneventful day at the Institute. He had woken early, the cold beginning to seep through his bones, and he had walked through the silent empty streets of Belsize Park in the dawn light, with only delivery boys and milkmen for company. The train was only half full, and James began to feel a sense of relief that in a couple of hours, he might have some answers.

He reached St. Gabriel's by mid-morning and headed straight for the porters' lodge, where he discovered that Haldane would be free around lunchtime. The middle common room would provide a place to keep a low profile until then, and so he climbed the ancient stone steps to the MCR where he took a seat looking out over the front quad, nodding greetings to a couple of postgrads who were enjoying their morning coffee. The papers had been delivered and he hurriedly scanned the front pages for some mention of the incident, but there was nothing. Again the terrible images of the previous day played in front of his eyes, and he was lost in thought when Dave entered, throwing his heavy raincoat over the hatstand and collapsing noisily into the armchair opposite.

'Jamie! Didn't expect to see you. We've only just finished clearing up from Monday. What a hell of a night that was! I lost sight of you around midnight. Did you slope off with that history girl, you old dog?'

'Well it turned out that we had a lot in common actually. She's a really nice girl....'

'Oh well. Anyway.' Dave had already lost interest in James's platitudes. 'But why're you here? Shouldn't you be doing whatever it is that you do at the Institute for International scrapbook making?'

He laughed loudly, and gave James a kick on his mud covered brogues.

'Actually there's been a bit of a turn of events there, David. In fact I've come to see Haldane for some advice. Can I fill you in on the details once I've seen the old boy?'

'Good God. I hope the gherkin-like Sue hasn't smothered the bearded librarian with her tea cosy hat'. Again, Dave's laugh boomed across the common room, drawing disapproving looks from the reserved coffee drinkers. He caught their eye and continued.

'You know, this lot make your Soho colleagues seem almost normal at times'.

Turning back to James, he spoke in a lowered

tone.

'Look, if there's any problem, you know you can stay in Summertown if you want to. Let me know if you need any help, Jamie. Let's meet at The White Horse after you've seen him'. Dave swept up his gaberdine, and tossing a copy of National Geographic at the postgrads, shut the door behind him with a great crash.

Noon approached, and James made his way round to Chapel Quad. Haldane had just returned to his rooms, and was both surprised and pleased to see him.

'Come in James and have a seat. How nice to see you. Can I offer you some refreshment? A sherry perhaps?'

'Actually, that would be very welcome,' James replied, trying to organise his thoughts, 'it would help to steady my nerves. I've come for some advice.'

'Well of course I'm only too happy to help if possible.' Haldane had brought a decanter from the back room and was filling a couple of glasses. James thought that his tone had become a little more circumspect. 'What's on your mind, James?'

'It's difficult to believe this, Mr. Haldane, but I witnessed a terrible scene yesterday. I returned to London, went to the Institute, and I found Jonathan, Mary and Sue - my colleagues - all dead.'

'I don't understand,' Haldane remained standing, the crystal decanter frozen in his hand, 'How could they be - dead?'

'They looked like they'd been shot. And I saw the killers. Luckily I escaped, but they followed me at first. I think I'm OK now. I don't think they saw my face.'

The blood drained from Haldane's face, and he sat heavily on his green leather chair. 'You say that Clarence is dead? Jonathan Clarence? You saw him? And he had been shot and killed?'

'Yes, I'm afraid so, and two of my other colleagues. It makes no sense to me. I think that the gunmen were Middle Eastern. I certainly heard Arabic voices just before I ran from the building. I was scared, and I made an anonymous call to the emergency services, but there's been nothing about it in the papers, and I began to think that the killers are terrorists, and that I should speak to Michael Godfrey first and take advice from him.'

'Slow down, slow down, James.' Haldane had finished his sherry and was pouring another. 'Let me try to gather my thoughts. You say that you heard the attackers, and they sounded Middle Eastern?'

'Yes. As far as I could tell.'

'But you haven't met with the police?'

'That's right. I thought that if I - I mean, we - could speak to MG first, then if there's another, more sinister dimension to all of this, then he can advise me.'

Haldane was clearly troubled, and sat in silence turning over this information, before walking around the desk to the phone, and placing it on the small drinks table between his chair and the chesterfield.

'Let's call Michael,' he said quietly, his throat dry with tension.

Haldane reached across the desk for his rolodex, and deftly turned the cylinder around to G. He picked out a card with Godfrey's details, and began dialling, the clear plastic dial turning painfully slowly as James waited impatiently. When the phone was answered, Haldane pressed the speaker button, and Godfrey's voice filled the study.

'Yes. Hello. Michael Godfrey speaking.'

Godfrey's voice sounded faint, and had an unfamiliar tremble.

'Michael. It's Anthony Haldane here. And I have our mutual friend, James Gunn here with me. You're on my new speakerphone.'

'Oh. I see. Very good. A speakerphone you say. Good afternoon gentlemen, and hello James. I'm glad that you've made contact.'

There was a silence as Haldane waited for James to recount his story. He took another sip of sherry and began.

'Mr. Godfrey. I thought I should speak to you first about an incident I witnessed, or at least the aftermath of an incident which I encountered yesterday. My colleagues are dead. They were shot. Can you help me to make sense of what I saw?'

There was a long silence. Haldane was becoming increasingly flushed, and James could feel beads of sweat forming on his own brow.

At last Godfrey replied, in a steadier and more deliberate voice.

'Anthony. James. I'm only too aware of what occurred yesterday. A horrible mess. Quite dreadful. And it's complicated. I'd like to take you into my confidence. Only then will I be able to explain what happened yesterday to you, James. But if you're willing to hear the truth, then you will have to assure me that you won't talk to anyone about this. That means friends, family, and whoever you happen to have a few drinks with in the pub. Anthony, you understand the way these things work. But can I trust you, James?'

James was filled with relief that MG could help, and was only too willing to offer his discretion in order to find out what had happened to his colleagues.

'I can do that sir,' he said clearly into the speaker. 'I need to know what happened.'

After another silence, Godfrey continued.

'Then thank you for your compliance. What I'm about to tell you is extremely sensitive, and I can only reiterate that it must go no further than the impressive, book-lined walls of your study, Anthony.

'So. As you know, we gather information into the Institute from our American friends at their London embassy. And as you also know, James, our esteemed late colleague Jonathan Clarence was solely responsible for using that information to organise consignments of foreign aid.'

After a pause, Godfrey went on.

'What you didn't know, James, was the nature of those consignments. Neither of you will have heard of a covert government operation which is engaged in supplying weapons to the Mujahideen; the anti-Soviet forces in Afghanistan. We call it Operation Cyclone. And I'm not talking about a few guns here and there. Last year we shipped thirty million dollars worth of armaments to the guerrillas. And our governments will spend another thirty million dollars this year.

'So far, so good. But then we come to the problem. What neither you nor I knew was that dear old Jonathan was not at all what he seemed. Jonathan, it turns out, was a quisling. A turncoat. A traitor. Somehow - and we don't know how - he was letting our Soviet friends know where and when consignments were due to be delivered. The Afghans began to suspect that he was leaking information, and we agreed to have a little fireside chat with him, to discuss whether there was anything, shall we say, that he wanted to tell us.

'And that is when the whole thing went off the rails. Incredibly embarrassing. Needless to say, I am under immense pressure. Of course I have disbanded the Institute.'

Haldane sat forward anxiously. James too, was unclear as to how the story had ended.

'Sorry MG, old chap. Not quite sure we understood you there, just at the last fence, you seemed to go round it completely.'

'Oh, yes. Terribly sorry Anthony. Mind's in a muddle as you can imagine. It's those damned Mujahideen idiots. Impetuous, uncontrollable amateurs.' At this, Godfrey's voice rose to as close to an angry tone as Haldane had ever heard him use.

'You see. They couldn't wait. The bloody fools killed him. It's a complete disaster. Innocent women as well. What a mess.'

Haldane sat forward abruptly. 'So it was done as revenge for his deception? So do we know how Clarence did it and when? Do we know who his contacts were? How was all of this arranged? With those answers,' he hurriedly added, 'one might console oneself that at least something constructive has come out of this.'

'That, my dear Anthony, is the most frustrating thing about this shambles. Bloody fools should have waited until we had some information. Some details. As it is, we have no clue as to how he was passing on information. Any trail of contacts died with him. And as to when he passed on the information, the only good thing about any of this is that we are pretty sure - no, we are definitely sure - that he hasn't passed on any data for a couple of weeks, thank the Lord, since the operation is continuing. In fact it's preparing for a major shipment in a few weeks.'

Haldane sat back, looking up at the ceiling and trying to digest the information. James on the other hand felt an anger growing within him, which he only just managed to contain. He was angry and confused by the revelation of Jonathan's treachery, but more than that, he was angry at the needless loss of Sue and Mary. Surely people couldn't just be allowed to be forgotten like this.

'But Mr. Godfrey. Sue's parents. Who'll let them know? Surely this can't just be swept under the carpet indefinitely? What about justice for her?'

'James, I can quite understand that you feel rather dreadful about the loss of dear Susan, and as for Mary, well she and I go back a long way. The trouble is that if this incident becomes public, then questions will be asked - quite rightly - and of course by pulling at a thread here and there, the entire garment would unravel. The world is unaware of just how much we and the Americans, the Saudis and even the Chinese, are engaged in supporting the Afghan resistance. The Russians may suspect it, but we have to do all we can to leave it just like that - a suspicion. As for Susan's family, I will speak to them, and explain that there has been a dreadful terrorist incident which remains under investigation. We will do all we can to provide financial and personal support to them.'

'I'm sorry,' James continued, regaining control of his ragged emotions. 'It's a lot to take in at once. The whole thing is incredible and horrible.' Then, suddenly thinking of his own situation, he added, 'What happens to me now, the job, the Institute?'

'Well James, as I may have mentioned, the Institute is being dismantled, literally, as we speak. The Americans and our own security people have analysed Clarence's things, without much success, and I'm afraid it's now time to close this distressing chapter. As for your own position, we have unused funds which will help you along until you find your next employment. We propose paying you a full three months salary right away, and you should receive that in your account in a couple of days time. And you don't need to worry about the men who followed you yesterday. The security services have apprehended them, and they are the focus of an intense diplomatic row, as you can well imagine.'

Godfrey's voice tailed off, and James could imagine the swivelling eyes behind his magnifying lenses searching for a point on which to focus. He sounded tired and beaten. 'James', Godfrey concluded, 'We're so sorry that you've been caught up in this terribly ugly affair.'

Suddenly, James also felt exhausted, his body a lead weight against the red leather of the chesterfield. Haldane also looked drawn and distant.

'Shall we leave it there, MG?', Haldane addressed the speaker in a subdued tone. 'Wishing you all the best, old man. Hope to see you sometime soon.'

'Yes, quite', Godfrey replied, 'I must dash now, A lot of jobs to see to. Bye chaps.'

They sat in silence for a full minute, and then James roused himself, and made to leave the study.

'Thanks for helping me with this Mr. Haldane. I'm glad I came, I'm glad I know the truth, but I just wish that none of this had happened.'

'James, it must be dreadfully hard to think that your friend Jonathan was not the man you thought he was. You know how I feel about the Afghan conflict. Having listened to MG, I'm encouraged to know that there's more to this country's position of principle than mere rhetoric. And at the same time, on a personal level, it must be devastating to think that one has been lied to by someone you trusted, and who has betrayed those principles.'

'Thank you Mr. Haldane. Thanks for your support. I think I had better head off now. I have to start thinking about the future, and I'll have to learn to live with what's happened over the past few days.'

James paused at the bottom of the staircase, where he used the public phone to call his father. He put on as calm and positive an air as he could muster, and reassured George that everything was fine from his perspective. He told him that he'd spoken to MG, who had confirmed his suspicion that there was some terrorist involvement, and that the investigation was ongoing. He couldn't go into any details, and so there was nothing more that James could tell him.

'I'm still worried about you, son', George replied,

with a mixture of relief and concern. 'Are you supposed to go back to that place as if nothing had happened? What're you supposed to do?'

'They're looking after me Dad. They've paid me for several weeks, and I'm afraid that there's no Institute to return to. I'll have to put my efforts into finding a long-term job but you know that was my main aim all along.'

'In that case - the best of luck. I'll tell Mum that they're winding the place down, but that you're fine money-wise. She can't wait to see you back up here at Christmas. Take care of yourself'.'

'Thanks Dad,' James replied with a sense of relief. 'I'm looking forward to that too.'

He walked slowly to the pub to meet Dave. As he made his way along Turl Street he glanced up at the three stags which stared back at him from the crest above the gates of Jonathan's old college. It troubled him that he had sensed nothing about Jonathan which might have given an indication of his true self. He had been a charming and intelligent companion. He had made light of his work, and had made James feel welcome. There was so much about the week that was hard to accept.

He began to rehearse a version of events which would satisfy Dave's inevitable curiosity. As he crossed Broad Street, he was still trying out different narratives, but as he entered the pub, his mind went blank. He would just have to make it up as he went along.

'Pint, James?', Dave was already standing at the cramped bar, savouring a pork pie, which dripped with mustard.

'Guinness please,' James responded as he took a seat towards the back of the narrow room, next to the welcoming fire. 'And I'll have one of those as well.'

Dave settled himself, balancing pies and pints on a small, brass-topped table. 'So what's all this about, Jamie. Have you sorted yourself out?'

'Indeed. I've cleared everything up. I've decided that I really need to focus on a long-term job, so I wanted to put the idea directly to Haldane. You see he got me the job at the Institute, and I thought it was only right that I keep him in touch with my thinking, rather than him hearing it second-hand.'

'That's very decent of you, James. What did he have to say?'

'Charming as ever. Was only too glad to have been of assistance, even for a short while, and wished me luck in the City, assuming someone will have me there.'

'Good decision, Jamie. I have to admit that the Institute always seemed a little fuzzy round the edges to me. Mind you, it's a shame that you won't be bringing more tales of the Institute to brighten up my day. Will you see the Sue girl again? You know I think you actually have a bit of a soft spot for her. Am I right?'

Dave nudged James's elbow, sending a piece of

pork pie spinning across the pub.

'She was, I mean she is, a really nice girl, but I don't think we have that much in common. I doubt if I'll be seeing her again.'

'Never say never, James. One cold winter's night, when you're sad, lonely and miserable, her unusually fine example of Peruvian headgear might turn out to be the best sight in the world.' Dave grinned broadly then turned to demolish the last of his pie.

James was relieved that his story had been so readily accepted, and he was not a little alarmed at just how easily he'd been able to create this alternative reality, as he liked to think of it.

'Anyway. I have some good news James. My supervisor tells me that the Faculty are impressed by my thesis, and it looks like I'll be Doctor Lawrence before too long. And St. Gabriel's want me to apply for the English Fellowship that's come up since our Research Fellow took up that position at Yale.'

'This is fantastic news, David. It couldn't be better. Here, let me get another round in. This we have to celebrate.'

And so the afternoon turned into early evening, the two friends enjoying each other's company, and gazing into the future, which looked very bright for Dave. And as the beers went down, James too felt his sense of optimism return. He would take a late train and tomorrow he would start afresh. He had sent another salvo of speculative letters to a range of City firms, and it just needed one of them to bite for him to land the job that he hoped would clear the mists surrounding his own future.

# CHAPTER 8 SQUARE MILE

Julia's fingers stabbed manically at the keys of the Olivetti, its bell rang and she threw the carriage backwards almost knocking the half-empty milk bottle off the kitchen table. Her article for *The Clarion* was a day overdue and she was determined to produce five hundred words by lunchtime. Her arresting title was: 'Why we should discount the polls showing the Liberal-SDP Alliance is ahead of us'. She had no real idea about why we shouldn't believe them, but she would write the article anyway, with much zeal, vigour and many capital letters.

James sat opposite, munching his fourth piece of toast and marmalade, and writing yet another letter to yet another broking firm. "I would be very grateful if you were able to meet with me, so that I could express my keen interest in person" he concluded, signing the A5 Basildon Bond notepaper, and brushing off a few errant toast crumbs before sliding it into its envelope.

It was a week since his visit to Oxford. He had taken the story he'd told Dave, and developed it a little for his housemates. They too had very few questions, although Julia was disappointed that he was focussing on his "capitalist ambitions, in a typically bourgeois manner," rather than "continuing to support the provision of foreign aid." If only she knew, he mused, as he watched her beat the typewriter into submission.

He had been circumspect about his three-month payoff, which obviously didn't make any sense if it was he who had decided to quit the Institute. Just less than nine hundred pounds had appeared in his bank account the previous Friday, and he was careful not to alter his frugal spending habits. He did, however, spend a day in Oxford Street replacing the interview suit, and buying a long navy wool coat at Marks and Spencer. He also walked to Liberty in Regent Street, and treated himself to a leather-bound Filofax, which he had read was set to become a 'must-have' item in the City. When he left the store he couldn't resist walking towards Piccadilly Circus, then along to Silver Street, and standing for a moment outside number 19. He watched as office workers from the lower floors came and went in a picture of complete normality. He felt very low as he travelled north in the tube, the train screeching and grinding its way past Camden Town, and he found it difficult to shake off this feeling of dejection.

The letter box rattled, bringing him back to the present. 'I'll get the mail', he called out, and picked up a handful of letters and circulars from the doormat. Two were addressed to him, and he quickly tossed aside the first, recognising the credit card logo on its envelope. But the other was unfamiliar, and to his delight he found it contained a polite reply to his letter and CV, and an invitation to an interview with Marcus Stringer, managing partner of Leclerc Proust, Stockbrokers. At last, this could be the breakthrough he was hoping for. The letter asked him to come to Leclerc's offices near the Bank of England in two days time.

He dressed carefully for the interview. Too loud a tie might suggest an unwelcome degree of overconfidence. Too dull a tie might suggest a reticence which was inappropriate for the job. In the end he decided to play safe, and donned his college tie, which said; establishment, confident but not flamboyant.

The offices of Leclerc Proust were tastefully grand. Sitting at the south end of Moorgate, they overlooked the north west corner of The Bank. An intricate stone carving above the high oak doors showed the symbols of prudence; a wolf, a lion and a dog, all three poised, it seemed to James, to pounce on those crossing the threshold.

James was asked to wait in a small wood-panelled room next to the ground floor reception. It was blandly furnished, with two uncomfortable seats on either side of a worn oak desk. Three rather faded hunting scenes did their best to add some colour to the austere surroundings. Suddenly, Marcus Stringer burst into the room, shook James's hand in a perfunctory manner, and sat down briskly, setting his wrist watch in front of him, which he adjusted so that it lay at exactly ninety degrees to the edge of the desk. Stringer was tall and thin, and his cheek bones seemed almost to protrude from his sallow skin. He wore a jet-black suit, white shirt with cutaway collar, and a black silk tie. His short black hair was clamped to his skull with gel, which glistened in the dull light of the room.

'So. Gunn. Scottish I see. What part?'

'I was brought up in Glasgow, Mr. Stringer, and I attended Edinburgh and Oxford universities.'

'Glasgow'. Stringer barked back. 'That means insurance companies. Banks. Fine history. Do you know the Glasgow branch of the Ogilvie family? Or the Sutherlands?'

'I'm afraid not, sir. I don't know anyone back home who's involved in finance.'

'What do you actually know about then, Gunn? Your CV here says you studied nineteenth century writers. What was the point of that?'

'It helped me to develop skills which I hope I can use to..'

'To what, Gunn?' Stringer interrupted, 'I hope that you're going to say 'make money'. Make money for our clients, and for the partnership. You do realise that's what this job is about, don't you?'

'Yes, of course I do. I know I may seem like a fish out of water, Mr. Stringer, but I'm bright, and with training I'm sure I could make a go of it.'

Stringer sighed and checked his watch. 'Look Gunn. The City is changing, and this place is changing. I have the unenviable task of dragging the benighted house of Leclerc and bloody Proust into the twentieth century. The floors above us are full of chinless wonders. Useless sons of lazy parents, who I wouldn't trust to park my bike. I know - you must be incredulous. Well it all has to change. The Americans are going to land here with their bloody computers and their fucking research, spouting their aggressive version of the English sodding language, and those chaps upstairs will wet themselves. I need to find chaps with brains and a bit of guts. Do you know how to work a computer, Gunn?'

'Not exactly sir,' James replied quickly, thrown by this unexpected outburst of candour, 'but a friend of mine in Oxford who studies physics uses one every day, I think.'

'Well. At least you *know* someone who knows about computers. That's a start at least, albeit a pathetic one. Look. I've read your CV. I want people like you. To me you're raw material which I can mould into a sharp-witted arrogant bastard. Are you up for that, Gunn?'

'Well, that's not exactly how the careers service at college described the role, but I need a job, and if you think I have the potential to..'

'Good. That's settled,' Stringer cut him off in mid-sentence. 'The only thing that you need to do now is impress the senior partner. Nobody gets hired here unless Percival Beloe has approved the decision. I'll take you up to his rooms and you can meet him.'

'Is there any advice you can give me? About Mr. Beloe I mean?' James asked, rising to follow Stringer, who had swept up his watch and was already half way out of the door.

'Yes. Try to keep a straight face. Don't show any surprise if he does something - how should I put this - fucking weird. And try to be yourself. It's a cliche, I know, but you don't want to come to this madhouse if it's not really your cup of poison. Believe me, Gunn, this place has claimed the minds and the souls of plenty of weak-kneed wankers along the way.'

'Right. Keep a straight face. Got it. Thanks Mr. Stringer. I'm very grateful to you for giving me the opportunity..'

'Yes, yes. I know, I know. Look - keep the thanks, and repay me by justifying my quite inexplicable faith in you by becoming basically competent in the job. That alone would make you stand head and shoulders above every other arse in this building.' Stringer raised his voice as they passed a group of employees who were lingering in reception. He surveyed them with utter contempt, and they looked away quickly to avoid his look of disgust.

Beloe's rooms were on the top floor. The building was a physical reflection of the hierarchy on which the partnership was arranged. The printers and post room were in the basement. The settlements clerks were based on the ground and first floors. Institutional broking was on the second and third, but managing private wealth took pride of place on the fourth and fifth floors. The sixth floor was dedicated to the partners, consisting of dining rooms and private meeting rooms, and the top floor was given over in its entirety to the comfort of Mr. Percival Augustus Beloe, Baronet.

Stringer showed James the doors to the senior partner's suite, and then retreated, wishing him the best of luck. James knocked, and waited for some response. He knocked again, and then heard a brittle command of, 'Come!'

He opened the double doors and walked into a vast room lined with bookshelves, and with several desks arrayed around the space, each heaped high with newspapers and research studies.

'Come!' the disembodied voice called again.

James was perplexed. There was no one in sight. And then suddenly, Percival Beloe's head appeared above a desk in the middle of the room. His hair stuck out in all directions like an Einstein caricature. He was a portly man of around fifty, and wore an ill-fitting pinstripe suit which shone at the knees and elbows with the wear and tear of years of service. A heavy gold watch chain was stretched tightly across a stained waistcoat which was visibly straining to retain its contents.

'Chewing gum. Lost it there. Found it, so all good

now. Delighted to meet you. I assume that you are Scrimgeour, the maths graduate from Cambridge.'

'No.' James replied carefully, 'I'm Gunn. English graduate from Oxford.'

'Bugger. Bugger. Bugger.' Beloe exploded, with such passion that the sea of papers and books littering his room seemed to tremble as if caught in a minor earthquake.

'What is the point of our HR department if they can't brief me properly on the simplest of things? What was the name again?'

'Gunn, sir. James Gunn.'

'You're Scottish!' Beloe exclaimed, as if discovering a rare fact. He had picked up a pair of pince-nez glasses, and was peering at James through their murky lenses. 'Do you know the Ogilvies?'

James thought about how he could develop this dead-end question into an engaging answer.

'Not as such. But I believe that my father knew a Captain Ogilvie in his regiment. He was in the Argylls.'

'Interesting!' Beloe suddenly seemed even more animated. 'Sit down here. Let me clear these files off the chair and you can tell me about him.'

Beloe sat down opposite James in a large ornate chair, the arms of which had been carved into a bear on one side, and a bull on the other, and he continued,

'My father fought on the Western front, and he used to talk about the Scottish battalions with great respect. I did my National Service of course. Happiest eighteen months of my life. But then, when papa died, I took over the helm of this creaking ship, just as he had taken over from his father before him. I had very little choice. But what, may I ask, brings you here? And while you ponder your answer, I am going to lie on the carpet. It's good for the spine, and I find that a recumbent position helps me to concentrate.'

Beloe lay at James's feet, eyes closed behind the antique glasses, hands folded across his chest as if he were laid out in a morgue.

James reflected on Stringer's advice, concentrated on one of the framed share certificates which lined the walls, and began.

'I've been studying words for six years, sir. And now I want to make a radical change of direction, and be trained in a job which uses numbers. Where there is certainty and objectivity, and an obviously right answer to a problem.'

Beloe was silent at first, and James actually wondered if he had dropped off to sleep. But then he opened one eye and looking up at James replied,

'That is an unusual answer, Gunn. I usually hear some nonsense about making fortunes on the stock exchange, or how some obscure family contact thought it was worth the applicant having a stab at broking, as if we're a stall at a fun fair to be enjoyed and then forgotten. Your answer is unusual, but unusual doesn't mean that it makes sense. I think you're talking bilge, but at least it's interesting bilge.'

Beloe considered for a moment, and then continued, 'I like you, Gunn. You're different. And depending on Mr. Stringer's views, I'd like to give you a chance. But first, I'd like you to meet the people in our St. James's office. It's a shop front for wealthy customers and I think it may be a good place for you to cut your teeth. Let me have a word with Stringer, and we'll write to you with our thoughts. Oh and by the way, I notice that you haven't asked about the salary. Do you think I should regard that as a good or bad thing?'

'A good thing?', James ventured.

'Agreed. It won't be much, you know, but according to your CV it'll be a little bit more than you've been earning recently.'

And then suddenly Beloe sprang to his feet, showing a surprising degree of athleticism, and ushered James from his room, promising that he would hear from him in a couple of days.

Stringer was waiting at the foot of the stairs, talking animatedly to two staff members. He darted over to James.

'Well?', he enquired.

'Good, I think,' James replied. 'He's going to write to me and suggested I meet the people in the West End office.'

'Excellent. That all sounds very bloody good. So I reckon it's au revoir!' Stringer turned back to the two brokers, and James could still hear his invective-filled stream of abuse as he crossed Moorgate and walked towards the Stock Exchange.

He strolled along Throgmorton Street, and stopped at The Arbitrager for a beer. Despite the early hour, the long, narrow bar was packed full of jobbers and brokers, downing the first of many drinks of the day. The room was buzzing with talk of markets and overnight news, and James was amused by the endless jobbing stories - convoluted and painfully detailed tales which always seemed to present the narrator in the best of lights.

In some ways the City was very different to the world of academia, but in many others he felt that coming here would mean exchanging one set of codes and traditions for another, and he was beginning to like what he saw. Could he be happy here, with this group of eccentrics? Would life in the City offer the sense of purpose which he was seeking? He was mindful of Stringer's words; if this was his future, he would have to grasp it with conviction.

The letter from Leclerc Proust duly arrived the following Monday, inviting James to their offices in King Street at the end of the week. So he spent the intervening days on long walks on the Heath, and reading the Financial Times in the warmth of the reading room at the Highgate Literary Institution. As Friday approached he began to feel confident about this second meeting, and on the morning of the interview he walked down from Green Park feeling very bullish.

The West End office was a lot friendlier and a lot less chaotic than the City version. A small team of experienced private client specialists were extremely welcoming and showed James the process for taking on clients. They were led by the flamboyant and highly respected office manager, Miriam Goldberg. She cut a dramatic and imposing figure, in her totteringly high heels, beautifully tailored Chanel suit, and her trade mark wide-brimmed hat, which looked like it had been magically transported straight from the Paris catwalks. She invited him to attend a client portfolio review, which he found quite absorbing. He liked the element of structuring and planning. This seemed like the kind of work he was looking for. His interest must have been evident, as Miriam went on to show him a variety of different accounts with more complex requirements and investments.

The morning passed quickly, and after a final discussion about the daily routine at the office, Miriam walked with James to the reception, promising that she would be sending a favourable report to her colleagues in Moorgate. And she went on to surprise James by confiding that despite her first in maths, and her reputation for analytical brilliance, her first love was literature. 'If all goes well, perhaps you might indulge me in discussing my favourite writers in our lunch breaks? We can start with Byron and work forward from there.'

‘Of course. I’d be only too pleased’ James replied, delighted that his degrees were going to come in useful after all, albeit in a way that he would never have anticipated.

As he made his way along King Street to St. James’s Square the winter sun broke through the grey clouds, and as he crossed Pall Mall the handsome buildings of the clubs and offices seemed to reflect his increasingly positive outlook. It was chilly but dry, and he decided to buy a sandwich and coffee, and walk down through Carlton Gardens to the George VI memorial where he could sit on the stone benches, have a late lunch, and enjoy the view over St. James’s park.

Seated in the shadow of the grand Nash terraces, he wrapped his new Marks and Spencer coat tightly around himself, and organised his lunch on the broad stone seat. How quickly his life had turned around. Today was Friday the thirteenth, just over two weeks since he had walked into the scene of devastation at the Institute. He had continued to comb the newspapers for some mention of the deaths, but still there was nothing. He had turned over Godfrey’s words a thousand times, asking himself if he should have acted differently, and he was still burdened by a sense of guilt that his colleagues had been caught in a web of deceit, and killed, while he had escaped.

He drew his copy of the FT from his coat pocket, and began flicking through its pages as he sipped the weak but scalding coffee. At first he didn't notice the cab drawing up on the Mall at the foot of the steps, and its two passengers settling up with the driver. The man and woman began to walk slowly towards him. He was tall and well-dressed in a black cashmere coat with a velvet collar. She was also tall, and wore an elegantly-tailored long dark blue overcoat, belted tightly around her narrow waist. Black tights covered her slim ankles, and her high-heeled court shoes added to her imposing stature. Her rich dark brown hair was cut beautifully in a wedge which fell just above the stiff white wing collar of her shirt. James was enthralled, and sat frozen, his coffee cup to his lips. She was lost in conversation with her colleague, and he heard her laugh as she came level with the bench. Her eyes were fixed ahead, and James was lost in their dark beauty. Her mouth was attractive, and he found himself smiling as her conversation became more animated.

That voice. It was familiar. But its tone was lower. And he knew that mouth and the unselfconscious way that she walked. He slowly placed the coffee cup on the stone bench, as his heart pounded and he felt a cold bead of sweat drip between his shoulder blades. He watched, captivated, as a doorman stepped aside from the entrance to Number 9 Carlton Gardens, and Sue Almond stepped inside.

# CHAPTER 9 RESURRECTION

James's heart raced as he carefully approached the anonymous entrance to the elegant town house. He tried to appear nonchalant, surreptitiously glancing into the ground floor rooms, but the blinds were drawn behind the heavy sash windows. There was no name plate on the door, no indication of what lay behind the serene exterior, and the doorman had the challenging bearing of a soldier or policeman rather than that of a concierge. James walked on and only stopped when he reached Pall Mall.

His mind raced with a confusion of thoughts. It couldn't be her. She was dead. He tried to rationalise his reaction. Sue had been in his thoughts as the woman walked past him. He wanted to think that she could still be alive. And so he wanted it to be her, and that was why he had reacted the way he had, to someone who had simply given the impression of Sue. This was really about him. He was still haunted by the scenes in the Institute.

He had to move on. He had to put the ghosts of the Institute behind him. And so, driven more by emotion than by anything at all rational, he decided there and then to wait for the woman to leave the building, and put to rest the insane notion that this was Susan Almond. 'As in nut', he said to himself, remembering their first meeting.

If the building was a typical office, she would leave around five thirty. He would walk up to Green Park, and then take a slow stroll through St. James's Park, and be back in Carlton Gardens by then.

By the time he had reached Horseguards Parade the sun was beginning to go down over Buckingham Palace, and the Guards Memorial cast long shadows at his feet. To his left The Foreign Office, and behind him The Ministry of Defence, took his mind back to the meeting in Haldane's office. He remembered Michael Godfrey's revelations of the UK's clandestine help for the anti-Soviet resistance. He wondered what schemes and plots were being hatched all around him right now, behind the hundreds of brightly-lit windows of the government offices.

Back in Carlton Gardens his feet began to feel numb with cold, and he wondered afresh about the sanity of his plan. But he had waited this long and so he was determined to see it through. Around five thirty the door of Number 9 began to open more frequently, as its occupants began to depart, walking down the steps to The Mall or rushing back towards Lower Regent Street. It was around six when his attention was drawn to a group of around eight men who left together and headed towards

Pall Mall. At the last minute he spotted the woman amongst them, a dark red cashmere scarf almost hiding her hair and neck. He followed the group at a distance as they moved towards Trafalgar Square and into Covent Garden. It was dark now, and the crowds of homebound office workers made it easy for James to retain a discreet distance, but also to have a longer look at the woman. He tried to listen to her as she attempted to be heard above the noise of the constant stream of traffic.

He dropped back a little as they approached Maiden Lane as it was narrow, less busy, and he might appear more conspicuous. About half way along, the group suddenly disappeared, and it was only as he walked past Rules restaurant that he saw them through the large windows, grouped around the bar. The room was brightly-lit and James was able to take a good long look at the woman as she slipped off her coat and scarf and handed them to the waiter. Underneath, she wore a crisply-tailored suit in a fine navy pin stripe, its pencil skirt and double breasted jacket accentuating her height and figure. James tried to imagine her face with Sue's large brown-framed glasses and with Sue's nondescript fair hair. If Sue had worn heels she would have been about the same height as this woman.

The top-hatted doorman was busy at the entrance to the restaurant, trying to give directions to a party of disoriented tourists, and so James was able to continue watching as the barman handed the woman a flute of champagne, and she toasted her colleagues. They had placed their briefcases behind the brass rail at the foot of the bar, and were now engaged in an animated discussion, and from time to time huddled closely to gain more privacy. The sommelier, dressed impeccably in a long white apron and black tie, worked his way discreetly around the group, offering refills from the bottle of vintage Lanson. As he reached the woman, she raised her glass to the bottle, and something bright reflected on her wrist. A silver charm in the shape of a crest with three red stars hung below the starched cuff of her shirt for a few seconds, and glinted in the lights of the restaurant, before she turned back to the men and the conversation.

James stepped back sharply, almost colliding with the group of tourists who were now striding purposefully towards the market. He half-stumbled into the bar across the lane from the restaurant, and taking a seat by the window he ordered a double Gordons and tonic, which he drained in one. Ordering another, his head began to spin with his discovery. If that were Sue, then who had he seen at the Institute? He hadn't actually seen the victim's face, although he had seen Mary and Jonathan. And if the sophisticated, beautiful woman in Rules restaurant was the real Susan, then who was the Sue he had known in Silver Street?

He ordered chicken and chips and took it back to the window. He could see the group moving into the heart of the restaurant, taking their seats below a large painting of a harbour scene. Sue sat with her back to the painting and below an ornate carriage clock, her dark hair lit on either side by lamps held aloft by classical statues. He could just see their first course being brought on large silver platters, an impressive array of seafoods accompanied by baskets of assorted breads. He looked down at his shrivelled chicken wings and limp chips, and re-focussed on the group who were now ordering wine, the waiters and sommelier busying themselves attentively around them. He hoped that they weren't planning several courses as he pushed the remains of his dinner to one side, ordered a pint of Guinness, and settled down with his newspaper to begin his vigil.

Around nine thirty he began to see movement around Sue's table as the waiters brought coats, hats and briefcases, and the group began to ease out onto the street, calling hearty goodbyes to the doorman as they made their way towards Charing Cross. Sue was the last to leave, accompanied by the tall man that James had seen her with at lunchtime. They stood close to each other on the narrow pavement and seemed to be engaged in an intense conversation, before he leaned over and kissed her chastely on the cheek, and strode off towards the Aldwych. Moments later a cab appeared, its yellow light and headlights bathing Sue in a bright glow as it came to an abrupt halt and she stepped lightly inside. James pushed the remains of his drink to one side and ran into the street, where a cab was drawing up at Rules to deliver a fresh group of diners. He leapt into its back seat and ordered the driver to follow the cab in front, which was now turning right towards the Strand.

He settled back into the leather seat, and watched the buildings of the Kingsway flash past as the cab picked up speed. He tried to form a plan for how he would confront her. What if she simply denied his claims? He continued to struggle with his thoughts as the cab turned right into Theobalds Road and headed north east towards Islington. James wasn't familiar with this part of town, which exhibited an increasing grandeur as he traveled north into Amwell Street. Sue's cab suddenly turned right into Myddleton Square, and stopped outside the looming edifice of St. Mark's Church. He asked his driver to pull over, settled up, and went cautiously into the square. Here the terraces of Georgian townhouses were even more imposing, exuding wealth and taste, their five stories set behind black railings which led up short flights of steps to handsome doors flanked by classical columns.

As he rounded the corner into the heart of the square he saw Sue walking towards number 74, a particularly beautiful town house. By the light of the street lamps he could see a glorious winter jasmine which tumbled from its upper floors and made an arch over the high drawing room windows on the first floor. He thought that she hadn't seen him, but as she was about to turn her key in the lock, she suddenly turned and confronted him.

'Who's there? Who are you? You're following me!'

James took a step forward into the light of the Victorian street lamp. He saw her recoil briefly before regaining her composure.

'It's me, Sue. It's James. From the Institute. I thought you were dead. I'm so pleased to see you.'

Her voice rose. 'You keep away from me! You're mistaken. I've never seen you before, and if you don't fuck off I'll call the police.'

'But Sue,' he took a step forward, 'Please help me to understand this. I know it's you. I saw your bracelet. Just talk to me and explain.'

In that instant her demeanour changed. Her look was more urgent, and her jaw tightened. She swiftly reached around to the door, turned the lock and had almost closed it behind her, when James, who had dashed up the steps instinctively, caught his right foot in the opening. Sue swung the door against his foot with a force that made him cry out in pain, but the door didn't close. Then all in one motion, she hauled the door backwards, James fell into the hall, and she pushed him forward, where he stumbled face-first into an ornate coat stand. She kicked the door shut, and calmly reached into her crocodile-skin briefcase, drawing out a Walther

PPK which she pointed directly at his head.

James recoiled at the sight of the gun, and stared back at her in terror as he clutched his bleeding nose.

'Walk,' she said, 'Right. Into the study.'

James limped forward into the large book-lined room. The richly-furnished study contained a large desk by the window, an antique drinks cabinet, two grand sofas on either side of a cabin trunk which served as a table, and two grey metal filing cabinets, which sat in dull contrast to the dark reds and purples of the curtains and furniture.

'Sit,' she said, pushing him towards a sofa, and continuing to train the pistol at the centre of his forehead. She reached across to the cabinet, picked up a napkin, and tossed it at James.

'Don't bleed on my sofa.'

James held the cloth to his nose, with his head held back to try to staunch the flow of blood. His right foot throbbed as the sensation began to come back. His gaze settled on a painting above the high marble fireplace. It was a study for Guernica, and despite his pain, he couldn't help wondering if the signature was authentic. Who was this woman who had come back from the dead, but was now changed out of all recognition? The Sue he had known didn't carry a gun and he was pretty sure that she didn't own a Picasso.

He lowered his head, and at last was able to take in the full beauty of the woman in front of him.

She had removed her jacket, and was leaning back against the desk. He tried once again to engage with her.

'Look. I don't know what this is all about, but I don't mean any harm. I was - no I am convinced that you're someone called Susan Almond, who I worked with until quite recently.'

'You said that she was dead. Do I look dead to you?'

James thought he detected the faintest creasing around her eyes as she spoke.

'On the contrary. You look very much alive,' he replied, his eyes returning to the Walther which was trained on him.

Without altering her gaze she leaned over to the drinks cabinet, picked up a decanter of whisky and poured a large measure into a crystal tumbler. Then she carefully placed the decanter and another glass on the chest in front of James.

'Scotch? Why don't you take your mind off these fantasies of yours for a moment. I have to make a call.'

She arched back over the desk without taking her eyes off him, picked up the receiver, and using the end of a fountain pen turned the dial slowly. The clicking of the dial was the only sound in the silence of the house, and then suddenly someone answered.

'It's Latham. Code two eight six.' After a short pause, she continued, 'Response code four nine five.' Another pause, then, 'I have to speak to the head gardener. It's important.' The voice at the other end of the phone sounded apologetic, and so she continued, 'Then try him on the secure line to the Nomads Club.'

There was another long pause, and then James could hear the muffled tones of a man's voice at the other end of the line.

'We have a little bit of a problem I'm afraid, sir,' she responded. 'I'm at home and I've been joined by Mr. Hartley. Isn't that just wonderful?'

James could make out the sound of a sharp response and then a silence.

'As you know sir, the contingency plans offer two alternatives. In one we invite Mr. Hartley into the garden, and in the other we say thank you and goodbye. What's your decision, sir?'

They both waited, motionless, and he could sense the tension run through her. Biting her lip, she looked away from James's eyes, preferring to focus on the whisky in his hand.

After what seemed like an eternity, her face relaxed, and she seemed to breathe more easily.

'Thank you sir. I can start the conversation but he needs clearance. I'm afraid that despite the late hour I'll have to bring him in. Can you send a car and someone to make sure that things tick along smoothly? Thank you. I'll see you around eleven thirty.'

She replaced the receiver, and moving round to

sit on the sofa opposite James she picked up the decanter.

'You need a refill, James,' she said, in a softer tone, pouring a large Scotch into her own glass. 'Here you are.' She placed the decanter back on the trunk between them.

'It's actually nice to see you, James. I didn't think I was going to see you again, and I must confess, part of me regretted that. Can I just say one thing, before we go on? I liked the way you were kind to Sue Almond. You're a nice chap, and I certainly never wanted to do you any harm.'

James felt a mixture of delight that she had acknowledged him, relief that he hadn't imagined the whole thing, and frustration at his bewildered ignorance.

'Why did you say your name was Latham?' He asked, pouring out a generous measure. 'And you have a gun. What the hell is all that about?'

'Because that happens to be my name, James. I'm Lucinda Latham. Pleased to meet you.' And with that she raised her glass to him in a welcoming toast. 'And don't worry about the gun. I use it only rarely'.

'So what about Sue? What about the home counties upbringing? What about the Oxford degree?'

'All a fiction, James. All except the degree of course.... I thought that much would be obvious. Sue was a fiction. A front. She was part of the alternative reality we created in order to progress the assignment, but you'll hear more about that soon. We're going on a short journey in about twenty minutes.'

'To see your boss?' James asked, trying to suppress his impatience. 'Why did you call him a gardener? You were talking in riddles. And if Sue was a fiction, then tell me about the reality.'

'Oh, the garden and the gardener names are just shorthand. Our main office happens to be in Carlton Gardens. But I guess you know that already. And I call the director general the head gardener. It's all silly schoolgirl stuff, but it'll make sense to you soon.

'As for me, I'm the second daughter of Lord Latham of Argyll and Bute. My upbringing was about as far removed from a middle class home counties one as you can possibly imagine. I was brought up by a series of nannies after my mother's death, and spent most of my childhood and school years in Switzerland where Daddy owns one of his larger properties.'

'And so then came Oxford. So what was your degree?'

'A first in PPE. And by the time I'd graduated Daddy had a new wife - perfectly pleasant, a bit dim, and not much older than me.'

'So, do you see much of them?'

'I used to spend my holidays with them on the family estate in Scotland. Down here in London he has his own house in Belgravia.'

'And so what about this place? It's pretty impressive.'

'Oh, this place is mine. Daddy bought it for me a couple of years ago. A purely commercial thing, you understand. Something to do with reducing inheritance tax liabilities.'

James was having to work hard to take in this whole new history. 'And the the furniture, the antiques?'

'Yes. There'll all mine, if that's what you're wondering.'

'And the painting above the fireplace?'

'Yes, it's what you're struggling to believe it is.' Lucinda smiled for the first time.

'Christ,' James breathed out, taking another large helping of whisky from the decanter. 'And so what about Julian? Was he a figment of your imagination as well?'

'Do you really think I'd get involved with someone as appalling as the fictitious Julian? Please! Show me a little respect, James!'

He smiled, but he still felt deeply annoyed at all the lies and deceit.

'That's good. I mean, I'm pleased that you're not with someone like him. So the guy you kissed goodbye at the restaurant - is he a boyfriend?'

Lucinda looked a little surprised at this, and sipped her drink. The pistol still sat in her right hand, but she had dropped it to the sofa. She had relaxed a great deal since the phone call, and since the whisky had begun to take effect.

'That's not really any of your business, James.' She replied tersely, looking away. But then she looked back at him and smiled awkwardly.

'But since you ask, no. He's not my boyfriend. Giles isn't interested in girls, as it happens. As for me, I don't really 'do' boyfriends. I work. I work some more. And then I come home to my gilded cage. And usually I don't spend the evening with a man, a decanter of whisky, and a pistol. Just in case you wondered.'

'Well thank you,' James replied, 'That is very good to know.'

They sat in silence for a moment. Their eyes met, and neither could think of the right words to continue the conversation. The doorbell rang relieving the tension.

'James, before I get that, can you just remind me how you recognised me in the restaurant?'

'Your charm bracelet, Lucinda. I was pretty sure it was you, but your college crest gave the game away.'

She thought for an instant, then replied firmly, 'I think it would be good if you didn't mention that this evening, James. Or indeed, ever.'

'That's fine by me, Lucinda Latham,' he replied, with a smile.

'Sorry about your nose,' she said, returning his smile, and walking towards the door.

'I was more concerned about the gun to be honest,' he called back as she disappeared into the hall, where he could now hear voices. Lucinda quickly reappeared accompanied by an impressively proportioned man, whose six foot frame looked like it could be composed exclusively of muscle. His arms and legs seemed too thick for his suit, and his bull-like neck strained against the collar of his shirt. James noticed the top of a regimental tattoo protruding a little over the collar, its black ink contrasting with the pale pinkness of his shaved scalp.

Lucinda slipped back into her jacket and coat, and introduced her friend.

'Harry, this is James, who's coming with us to the Gardens. James, this is Harry, a special friend of mine who works in insurance.' She grinned. 'He ensures that things work out without any fuss. And now I think it's time we were off.'

Lucinda went down the steps to a waiting car, where the driver was holding the rear passenger door open for her.

'You first, James,' Harry gestured to him to stand up and follow her. He continued in a low growl, 'I see she gave you a tap on the nose, mate. Given we're talking about Miss Latham, I'd say you got off lightly. Fold up that napkin neatly, pal, and put it back on the cabinet before we go. Miss Latham is very particular about tidiness.'

James was ushered into the back seat alongside Lucinda, with Harry in front alongside the driver. They travelled in silence, retracing the route that he had taken in the cab. The Jaguar saloon was spacious and Lucinda stretched out her legs then crossed them under her long coat. From the crocodile-skin briefcase she produced a bottle of Opium, and absent-mindedly applied the rich and heady scent behind her ears and on her wrists. James tried to catch her eye, but she was gazing out at the buildings of the Strand as they sped past Simpsons and then The Savoy.

'Lucinda,' he started, 'One more question. Why did you call me Mr. Hartley back there?'

Lucinda turned to him, and with an embarrassed smile replied, 'We called you L.P. Hartley. It was your code name.' Seeing James's puzzled reaction she continued. 'You're the one that studied literature, James. You can work it out. What was the name of Hartley's best known novel?'

'The Go-Between,' James breathed out softly, as the car swept into Carlton Gardens, and came to a halt outside Number 9.

# CHAPTER 10 THE GO-BETWEEN

A concierge ushered James into a waiting room just off the grand hallway of the Victorian mansion, while Lucinda and Harry went through to the main office overlooking the park. James was still shocked by Lucinda's story, the gun, and the pace of events, but he began to regain his composure, assuming that if these people had wanted to cause him any harm it would have been easy to do so by now. He would be patient and hear them out.

Harry appeared after several minutes and led him into the office. The room had an austerity which surprised James. Wood-panelled walls on three sides and full length windows on the fourth looked out over Horseguards Parade, and across to Downing Street. Apart from the lights from the traffic on the Mall, the room was lit only by two low bankers lamps which sat either side of a large mahogany pedestal desk. Harry gestured to James to take a seat in the simple wooden chair facing the desk, and then retreated to a seat in the shadows of the room. A door from the deeper recesses of the building opened, and Lucinda reappeared with a thin stick of a man whose gossamer-like presence moved silently across the Persian carpet. He sat down behind the desk facing James with his child-like back to the towering windows. Lucinda took a seat by the side of the desk and introduced the slim figure as Mr. Horace Waft.

'Good evening, Mr Gunn,' he wheezed in a voice which was like wind passing through a bank of reeds. 'I'm sorry to trouble you with a few pieces of necessarily tedious bureaucracy, but in your unusual circumstances, it is advisable from your perspective that you comply with certain formalities, the protocols regarding which have unfortunately been somewhat clumsily disregarded in your case in terms of their correct sequencing, but to which we are able to return given a willingness to do so on your part, assuming that is, indeed, your wish?'

James looked towards Lucinda hoping for some elucidating signal, but she simply smiled back at him, quietly tapping the crest of her bracelet with a polished red finger nail.

'I wonder, Mr. Waft, if I could ask you to be a little more specific?' he replied.

Waft pursed his thin lips, and adjusted the half-moon spectacles which sat on the sharp bridge of his hooked nose, giving the impression of a short-sighted curlew.

'But of course, Mr. Gunn. Despite your unorthodox introduction into the functioning of the department, on which point, you will note that I am remaining non-specific - and indeed if pressed on the actual existence of an entity giving meaning to the noun used, I would reserve my right to disown said usage - I think it advisable that I continue with our conversation as if we were meeting in a more orthodox context, (orthodoxy in this instance being a relative term), and that I should aver that you may be interested in having a discussion with us about specialised appointments in government service which occasionally arise in the field of foreign affairs.'

'So you're saying that I've rather stumbled into the situation I find myself in, but we can continue as if I were having a job interview?'

Waft considered this, drew a deep breath and said, 'Yes.'

James hesitated, expecting this short answer to sit at the entrance to another linguistic maze, but Waft sat silently, studying him over the slim spectacles.

'So what do I have to do now?'

Waft sat back and took a manilla file from one of the desk drawers, placing it in front of James. 'The Official Secrets Act, Mr. Gunn. If you are agreeable, you might wish to sign page four where I have taken the liberty of printing your name in advance.'

James scanned the short document, accepted the pen which Waft offered with a bony hand, and signed with a flourish. Now he would get to the heart of the matter. Now he would find out exactly what he'd been part of.

'Goodnight, Mr. Gunn. It's been a pleasure to meet you, and thank you for your helpful disposition and conclusiveness.' Then to James's surprise, Waft picked up the file and stepped quietly into the shadows. He barely heard the door shut behind him.

'How are you feeling, James?' Lucinda stood and leaned over the desk. He caught the scent of her perfume, and for a moment he relaxed.

'I'm fine, Lucinda. I'm keen to get on with whatever this is. Do you interview me now?'

'You flatter me, James. Thanks, but no I don't. I'm going to fetch the Chief who'll paint the rest of the picture for you.'

'Fine. You mentioned his club on the phone, so I have a pretty good idea of who to expect.'

And just as James had anticipated, a couple of minutes later Michael Godfrey's stout frame sat opposite him, the desk lights reflecting off the impenetrable lenses of his glasses, offering only fleeting glimpses of the eyes which strained behind them.

'Hello, James,' his soft tones were friendly and oddly reassuring. 'I had thought that our paths were unlikely to cross again, but here we are. And you've managed to meet Lucinda, which is all very clever of you, I'm sure. And you have lots of questions, and so now we propose to tell you all. You've signed Mr Waft's bits of paper, and so we can have a bit of a heart-to-heart, as it were, and at the end of it you might decide to rethink your City job plans, and consider getting a little closer to me. Oh, and of course, more familiar with Lucinda.'

At this, James heard Lucinda stifle a cough.

Godfrey's impressive eyewear turned a little towards her, paused, and then returned in the general direction of James. He leaned forward, and producing a pipe asked Harry if he happened to have a light. Harry emerged from the darkness, and with a motion which looked well-practised, held a long match in front of MG whose face lit up with delight when the pipe began to produce a cloud of sweet smoke from the Sobranie tobacco.

'Let's start at the beginning, James.' Godfrey leaned back in his chair, laying one hand across his ample waist while holding the pipe close to his lips with the other.

'Welcome to the Government Communications Bureau, also known as the Secret Intelligence Service, MI6, and to some, "The Circus".'

'I've been involved with the service one way or another for a very long time, James, but I only took over the job of Chief at the beginning of this year. It's a long story, and probably one for another time, but it was felt that some changes were needed within the service to deal with the KGB's plans significantly to step up the efficiency of their special operations task groups. In my time in the field, I've gained a lot of experience of how the Russian special ops. groups function. I've also spent many exhausting months in our Kabul station, and during that time my main local adversary was a man called Oleg Komarov. As I will explain, all of these factors combined to make me particularly fit for the role of Chief of the Service.'

James began to put the pieces together.

'And so I guess that my situation links somehow to the operation that you told Haldane and me about - Operation Cyclone - the supply of weapons to the Afghan resistance? It's a part of the world that you know well.'

'You're warm, James,' Godfrey replied, 'But let me explain exactly how Operation Cyclone has been managed. Let's start with our old friend Anthony Haldane. I find myself sitting here pondering when it was that we first realised that he was handing information to the Russians. Was it five years ago? Or maybe seven?'

James leaned forward, disturbed by this casual assertion that the Rector of St. Gabriel's was a traitor. 'You must be mistaken, Mr. Godfrey. This can't be correct. Haldane is, as you know, one of the most outspoken supporters of our government and our country's values, and his reputation is impeccable.'

'Exactly,' Godfrey continued, 'And that made him very good at what he was doing, until we began to suspect him - a little coincidence here, the hint of a suggestion from a defector there - it all began to add up, and eventually we gained proof through our people in Moscow that Haldane was indeed engaged in passing sensitive information to his KGB contacts.'

Godfrey leaned forward, producing a cloud of pipe smoke which swirled in blue and white wisps in the desk light.

'So we had to decide how to deal with Haldane's errant behaviour,' Godfrey continued, 'and we decided that because he had no suspicion that we knew of his underhand antics, as it were, that we should find a way to use him. To exploit our knowledge and his disloyalty at the same time.

'And so we came up with a plan. We would use a double agent - one who is on the KGB payroll, but is working for us - to use Haldane as his messenger. You see, James, direct contact between an agent and his ultimate handler can be dangerous, and agents often prefer to use a reliable middle man - someone they can trust, and who is above suspicion - to pass secrets on to the man at the top, the senior operative. That way the agent can operate efficiently without ever knowing the identity of the senior KGB officer, which means that if his activities are discovered, he has less to tell us. He knows that we are less likely to - how shall I put it - be more persistent in our enquiries.'

'OK. I'm with you so far.' James sat back, willing to accept for the moment the accusations about Haldane, in order to see the full picture. 'But even if Haldane is involved as a go-between, as you say he is, how does that benefit you?'

'Precisely the right question, James.' Godfrey continued, 'And that is where we come to Operation Cyclone. You see we have been waiting patiently to exploit Haldane for some time. On occasion we've fed him various low-level titbits of information through various routes, and then sat back and watched as the Russians have acted on the data, and that has confirmed our suspicions.

'But we had been saving him up for a bigger purpose, and we decided that Cyclone would be his big moment. We made sure that our double agent had access to details of the operation, and that our agent asked Moscow to sanction his passing on those details via Haldane. You remember how Haldane denied that he knew Jonathan when you and I first met in September? Of course I knew he was lying.'

'Okay,' James replied. 'Now you mention it, he did make a mild show of the fact that he hadn't met Jonathan. I think I can see where this is going.'

'Indeed.' Godfrey replied, and continued. 'And so we began to feed Haldane accurate descriptions of arms cargoes, the times and places of their delivery and so forth, but always the details of small consignments of older equipment which we could afford to lose and which couldn't do much damage to the Soviets in any case. And so the Russians came to trust the process. They were happy that Haldane was passing on the information that their agent was unearthing, and happy that it was genuine. They were happy - but more importantly - we were happier.

'You see we had them where we wanted them; fully trusting the source and the quality of the information. And so the next and final step was simply to inform Haldane and his handler of a major consignment, which is planned for next Saturday, the 21st. But that information, as I'm sure you've already worked out, is false. It will act as a major decoy, dragging the Soviet forces to one location, while we deliver a huge consignment of arms and equipment to a completely different place, a consignment which we believe will help to alter the course of the Mujahideen struggle in their favour.

Godfrey paused, his head settling into the folds of his chins, and took a number of short draws on his pipe, filling the room once again with a dense fog of smoke.

'Very clever,' James said after a pause. 'I can see how all of that worked, and I can also see that there were actually two go-betweens in the chain. I can see that Jonathan was the source of the information, and how his involvement with the Americans put him in the perfect position to inform the KGB about Operation Cyclone. And I can see how it would have been of benefit to all parties for his relationship with Haldane to be covert. And so I guess that that's where I fitted in. The notes, the diagrams, all the nonsense about battle plans in the

Crimea. You said when we first met, Mr. Godfrey, that I was going to have a role akin to that of a bag carrier. I didn't realise that you meant that literally.'

James paused. He was fascinated by the operation which Godfrey was unveiling. But he felt foolish. He had been used by these people, and he had been fooled by Haldane. And although he could see the positive ends, he baulked at their underhand means. But more important than his wounded pride was the truth of what had occurred at the Institute and why. He looked at both Godfrey and Lucinda, and in as controlled a voice as he could manage, continued.

'So if Jonathan - if that is his real name - was the double agent, that means that you and he were in control of the entire plot all along. So leaving aside just how pissed off I feel at the moment, let's concentrate on him. I'm hoping that he, too, is alive and kicking?'

Godfrey turned to Lucinda for help, dropping pipe ash down the front of his long-suffering waistcoat, then turned back. 'James, I am delighted to respond very much in the affirmative. Did you manage to contact him, Lucinda? Is he popping by this evening?'

'He should be here any moment, Chief,' Lucinda replied, rising and bringing another chair from the shadows.

'And I think we all deserve a nightcap when he arrives, don't you?' Godfrey continued. 'Harry,

I think we still have some of the 1958 Hermitage cognac in my office. The year you were born, James. I think that would suit us all very well. Go off and dig it out Harry, there's a good chap, and we can all toast Lucinda, Jonathan and Mary. All well and in the pink. And when Jonathan arrives we can explain why we had to stage a little amateur dramatics for your benefit, James, and for the benefit of our friends in Moscow.'

'I'm relieved that they're all well, but forgive me if I don't burst into spontaneous applause. Your methods are outrageous.'

Godfrey's tone hardened. 'Convincing and effective, is how I prefer to think of them, James. And don't forget that it was Haldane who introduced you to the Institute, not us. You're here this evening because of him. We're actually being jolly decent by welcoming you on the inside.'

Godfrey produced another billow of smoke and then continued in his more familiar, avuncular tone. 'Please don't take against us so, dear chap. Bear with us, and who knows, you may even want to join in.'

Harry returned carrying brandy glasses on what looked like a tea tray, and a tall bottle whose contents shone a deep golden in the dim light. 'Oh what excellent work, Harry,' Godfrey's attention shifted to the brandy. 'Let's all enjoy a well-earned libation. You as well, Harry. Don't be shy.'

As Harry was pouring the drinks, the door from

the inner offices opened, and Jonathan strode into the room, much to Godfrey and Lucinda's delight. 'How lovely to see you, Jonathan,' Godfrey said, half rising from his chair with an awkward struggle. He shook hands, as did Lucinda, with the tall and elegant man whom James could now inspect in more detail as he came closer to the desk lights. Gone were the beard and moustache. The hair was now blonde and arranged in a severe side parting. His wire spectacles had been exchanged for large, stylish frames, and his clothes were no longer a tweed and corduroy confection. Now he was dressed in a perfectly fitted Savile Row suit which in the dim light looked like a dark charcoal. A pristine white shirt with a Prince of Wales collar and a silk tie in cobalt blue completed the suave look.

'James. It's good to see you again,' he said, holding out a hand across the desk. James was delighted to see his old colleague, and shook hands warmly, before reminding himself that he was not supposed to be best pleased with his role in the story so far. He suppressed his enthusiasm, they all sat, and Godfrey continued, sipping his brandy as he spoke.

'So now that we have Jonathan here, I'd like to invite him to carry on the tale. I'd just finished explaining to James about how we conveyed the disinformation regarding next Saturday's operation.'

'Delighted to fill in the gaps, sir.' Jonathan began in his familiar charming manner, which James couldn't help but admire. 'My story really starts, I guess, when I was in Paris working for my postgraduate degree. I'd studied Russian history at Oxford, and was combining Russian language and history studies at The Sorbonne. I had a passing interest in politics, and fell in with a group of students who I thought were incredibly fashionable - experimental jazz, drinks at Les Deux Magots, pretending to understand Sartre and Malraux - you know the form. A lot of pretentious nonsense, really. But I was really happy, because I was accepted for what I am. You see James, as it happens, I bat for the other side, and I was able to be myself in Paris, whereas I'd been used to leading a double life before then. Perhaps that whole experience of living a life in secret explains why I felt confident about making the career decisions I made next.

'Anyway, it was during an evening with the existentialists, as I'd begun to call them, that I was approached by one of the visiting tutors, a chap who'd only been in the faculty for a couple of months. He was called Komarov, and he was completely charming. After sounding me out on a couple of evenings, he popped the question. How did I feel about the way Britain was changing? Thatcherism was creating social problems which would take years to remedy. The system was broken, and The Iron Lady would prove to be made of softer stuff in the long run. At that time I had planned to apply for work in international relations, and he encouraged me in that direction. And why didn't I work for him?

I would be briefed, looked after very well financially, and protected. All I would have to do is get into a position where I could gain access to 'useful' data. He would ensure a safe and discreet way of my passing that information on. What could be simpler?'

Jonathan paused, and took a sip of brandy. 'But the trouble about his plan was that unknown to Komarov, I had already had discussions with MI6 about using my Russian skills in one of our embassies in the Middle East. One of my Oxford tutors had put me in contact with a young guy called Francois MacNeill. Half French, half Scottish. He was working in the British Consulate in Paris. Francois was himself working for the service, and he'd been briefed to sound me out. I was enthusiastic, and had signed up for deferred entry on the conclusion of my degree. We began to be careful about meeting in public, in case Komarov or his agents were watching, but Francois knew a little restaurant on Rue Monsieur le Prince in the 6th, where the proprietor looked out for him and his contacts from the Consulate. We met there regularly and I told him about Komarov's approach. Francois could see the enormous potential for having someone placed close to Komarov, who could feed false information back to his people. And because of Komarov's involvement, Francois went straight to MG.'

'You said that you'd known Komarov in Kabul, Mr. Godfrey, but what is his role in the bigger picture?' James asked.

Godfrey took up the story from Jonathan. 'We'd been following Komarov's progress after his time in Kabul. He's a naval captain, first rank, and one of the KGB's most able agents. He rose up through the organisation, moving from active field work to recruitment roles, and then into strategic planning. The Soviet special operations units were creaking with the weight of tired thinking and stultifying bureaucracy, and we knew that Komarov was going to be promoted in order to modernise their structures. In August of this year he oversaw the regrouping and re-shaping of the KGB under a new and powerful unit named Vympel, or 'the flag unit'. He's taken all the best of the old units and created something new which will prove a more dangerous and elusive adversary than we've had to face for many years.

Godfrey took another drink, and continued. 'And so we come to the deaths in the Institute. We decided that if we could convince Haldane that we were unaware of any passing of information after mid-October, and that we could make him believe that the misleading communication on the day of your viva had not been detected, then it would be best if we gave the impression that Jonathan had been eliminated by reckless members of the Mujahideen. We could try to stage it so that the Russians would believe that they had lost a valuable agent in Jonathan, but that they still had useful information about the forthcoming arms drop.'

He contemplated the drifting cloud of pipe smoke for a moment, then continued, 'Of course it would be remiss of me not to thank you for the part you played, James. You see, we were pretty sure that you would visit Haldane to try to make sense of what you'd seen. It was your completely natural and authentic reaction which persuaded him of our 'alternative reality'. Our three-way telephone conversation drew as perfect a reaction from Haldane as we could possibly have hoped for.'

Godfrey placed his glass carefully on the desk, and turned to Jonathan, who continued,

'Of course when it becomes clear to the Russians that they've been deceived, and that I was part of that deception, they would have come after me themselves. But by staging our little play, we have spared them the effort. As far as they're concerned, James, I no longer exist.'

Godfrey picked up the story.

'We also felt that Komarov's new position as the head of Vympel made life too difficult for Jonathan in his current role. Komarov knows him personally, and was involved in what he thought was his recruitment, and so here was another good reason for his disappearance. Jonathan has no ties here in Britain, and so we agreed that it would be best for him to assume a new identity. And we're delighted to say that as from next month he will become head of counter intelligence for Eastern Europe at the CIA's headquarters in Langley, Virginia. And many congratulations on your splendid elevation, Jonathan.'

Jonathan leaned across the desk and placed his glass on the tea tray. 'That's very kind of you, Chief, and of course by then our little ruse will have played out, and our chaps will have delivered the biggest consignment of materials to date to the Mujahideen.' Turning to James he continued, 'So far we've been shipping fairly small stuff - ex-Indian army Lee Enfield rifles and basic radio equipment and so on. But next week will see explosives, limpet mines, the latest radio equipment, blowpipe missile launchers, and around three hundred missiles delivered into the hands of the Afghan resistance. And the Russians will be waiting to intercept the equipment at a site about one hundred miles from the actual drop location.

'And sorry again James, about all the subterfuge. Our 'play' began the day before your arrival at the Institute, when I assumed my disguise, and Lucinda chose to go one step further, and adopt a whole new identity. We thought that after the 'deaths' we wouldn't see you again, but that our disguises would mean that it wouldn't have mattered if we did. So I'm rather impressed that you were able to track down Lucinda. But none of that matters now. What matters is that we're all in one piece, and with luck, the operation will be a success.'

'Yes, it's all rather good, don't you think, James?'

Godfrey's gaze shifted to the desk in front of him. 'Yes, rather a pleasing design. A regular shape, etcetera. A satisfying arrangement all round...' Godfrey's voice began to tail off.

They sat in silence for a moment, then Godfrey appeared to experience a surge of energy.

'Right chaps. Enough for one night, I think. Terribly late. We ought to take a break and I'm sure that James will want to have a ponder. A period of rumination and reflection, as it were. I propose that we have a bit of a rest tomorrow, and then meet here again on Sunday morning. By then I will have formed my thoughts around how we might take things forward, and I will have some suggestions that may be to your advantage, James. I'm indulging in my customary Sunday lunch at the club, and so that will fit together perfectly. So good night to you all. I must dash. A few bits and pieces to do before I'm finished here.'

Godfrey rose with some difficulty, and shuffled out of the room and into the depths of the building, his pipe a small red glow as he walked into the shadows.

'Right. I'm off, Lucinda,' Jonathan said briskly. See you both on Sunday, and once again James, it's great to see you and to be able to talk openly. Have a good Saturday.'

Jonathan closed the door behind him, and Lucinda asked Harry to organise a car to take her and James to North London.

'The driver can take you up to Highgate after he drops me off,' Lucinda suggested as she swept up her coat and walked out towards the Gardens. Harry held the door of the Jaguar open for Lucinda, and she and James settled into the luxurious seats. James was beginning to feel a creeping exhaustion, but his mind was racing.

'Lucinda; why do you think Haldane chose me? It's obvious to me now that he thought I would make a perfect messenger.'

Lucinda thought for a moment, fiddling with a diamond earring, and leaned a little closer to him.

'He's a clever man. I think he saw someone who didn't come from money, unlike a lot of your fellow students, and so someone with no financial safety-net, who basically needed a job.' Her tone softened and she continued, looking out at the empty city streets, 'And I think that you're a little bit innocent. You're not cynical. In fact you're very trusting. And you're open-minded. He'd probably worked out that you're fairly apolitical, that you're not wedded to any cause or doctrine, so you'd be willing to work in an organisation like the Institute, without asking too many questions, or being put off by its obviously establishment bias.'

'You make me sound naive. A bit of a fool,' James replied, in a voice which was tired and resigned.

'Not at all, James,' Lucinda responded quickly. 'I think of you more as an adventurer. Someone who's not constrained by their background and beliefs. I think it's quite romantic actually. And I would be surprised if the Chief didn't think so as well.' She laughed at herself, 'Apart from the romantic bit of course.'

They had arrived in Myddleton Square, and stopped outside number 74. Lucinda gathered her briefcase and waited for the driver to come round to the kerbside to open her door.

'See you on Sunday, James.' Her tone was professional and direct once again. 'Be careful not to go alarming any young ladies before then.' She grinned, patting the contents of her briefcase, and sprang up the steps into the townhouse without looking back.

The driver turned into Upper Street and along Holloway Road, the streets lit by the countless street lamps and the changing reds, yellows and greens of the forests of traffic lights. He would take his time tomorrow to think over the evening's events and revelations. It seemed like a lifetime ago that he had been interviewing for the broking job. And now, depending on the outcome of the discussion on Sunday, a whole different role might be opening up for him. He thought about Lucinda's comments and found that he couldn't get her image out of his mind. She seemed to like him. She was positive. And he was going to be positive on Sunday. He remembered that conversation with Haldane on their first meeting. He *was* going to take sides. It was time for him to make a commitment.

# CHAPTER 11 COMMITMENT

James was woken the next morning by Steve thumping on his door to remind him that they'd arranged to go to the match that afternoon. As he came to and threw on some clothes, he tried to work through each part of his role as the go-between, and each element of the plan that Godfrey had recounted. It was easy to get lost in the detail. What mattered was the bigger picture, and whether the Service was the career that had eluded him so far - something that he could commit to. He'd felt enthusiastic last night, but now in the cold light of a November morning he wasn't so sure.

Steve was already excited about the match. An Arsenal obsessive, he became so tense ahead of games that he could barely eat. And now here they were in the Prince of Wales, Steve regarding his half eaten steak pie with nervous impatience while glancing repeatedly at his watch. The dark wood-panelled walls of the fine old pub gave a warmth to the atmosphere, as did the landlord's young family who carried the empties past the wood fire to the little bar. James was revelling in the cosy familiarity of the place, as he methodically finished off his chicken and chips and downed the last of his Guinness.

On the bus to Highbury James asked Steve if he had any experience of dealing with the Intelligence Services.

'Odd question, James, but I always wondered if your time at the Institute had given you a taste for all that stuff. No, is the answer. I'm strictly on the above-board economic side of the business. But I do have some old Cambridge pals who're involved, mostly overseas. If you're asking my opinion, I'd say go for it if you get the opportunity. My group in the Treasury makes decisions which affect millions of lives, but all of our planning and efforts would go down the drain if State Security wasn't robust. I'm not just talking about the obvious threats; in the future, life will be about bloody computers and we'll need to worry about all sorts of bastards hijacking the ones we use, the communications we depend on, and the way all of that technology drops money into the laps of criminals. If we lose control of that lot, then we're all fucked.'

'Right,' James replied, 'I get it. It's not just a twilight world of portly men smoking pipes and talking in riddles, and people drawing guns on you when you least expect it. You're saying that the whole labyrinthine effort might actually do some good.'

The jumble of buildings on the Holloway Road flashed by them. The giant art-deco cinema, the

Nag's Head, the Victorian-tiled entrance to the underground.

'James. We're playing Everton in twenty minutes. If you're having an emotional crisis - where am I, what am I doing, where am I going - all of that kind of stuff, then can I just suggest that we park it, and reconvene at ten to five, when I will either be wonderfully receptive, or I will be too miserable to speak.'

James looked closely at Steve. The veins stood out on his forehead as he tightened the red and white scarf around his neck. James agreed that the time for serious discussion was probably not now, and, depending on the result of the match, possibly not today.

They pushed their way off the packed bus and walked past Drayton Park to the stadium. They took their places in the North Bank, their bodies jostled backwards and forwards as the crowd moved in reaction to the movement on the pitch. Steve was on a different plane, in a different world, his every sense tuned to the ebb and flow of the game, and to the reaction of the crowd.

But although James also moved in unison with the seething mass, his mind was elsewhere. Lucinda. Jonathan. Godfrey. Could their world become his? His mind had been full of vague ideas and sketchy thoughts about his future. He hadn't had to focus on reality until he had met Stringer and Beloe. And now Godfrey seemed to be offering an alternative way forward.

He had always thought that life would be about making very considered decisions about the future. A carefully designed balance sheet for each step in life. But here he was, trying to form a clear plan amidst a deranged crowd of twenty-five thousand fanatics. Perhaps this was the reality. Perhaps a balance sheet can take one only so far, and the rest is down to instinct. And his instincts told him that he should commit to Godfrey and his world which lay just beneath the surface of the one we know. He felt that sense of wellbeing that comes with the making of a decision; the joy of putting the confusion of debate to one side, and choosing a path forward. He felt a sense of self-assurance borne out of the decision itself, and when Arsenal scored he joined in the ecstatic cheering, his voice adding to the deafening volume.

An hour later, buoyed on a sea of red and white, the strains of 'One nil to the Arsenal' ringing in their ears, James and Steve joined the crowd as it swept along Holloway Road, and finally made the steep climb up Highgate Hill. Passing the stone figure of Whittington's cat at the foot of the hill, he thought about his own return to the city tomorrow to begin to shape his destiny.

It was another cold but sunny morning as he walked through a quiet Regent Street to Carlton Gardens. Godfrey was waiting for him in the hallway wearing an outfit which was more fitting for the country than the town. Billowing mustard yellow trousers were topped by a dark green hacking jacket in a tweed so coarse that it looked as if it had been pulled off the loom prematurely. A checked waistcoat and elaborate watch chain completed the ensemble.

James had chosen to stick with his interview suit and he felt somewhat overdressed, but he relaxed when Lucinda arrived dressed in heels, an expensive-looking black trouser suit and a dark red silk shirt with a pie-crust collar. And Jonathan was also looking as smart as he had in the early hours of Saturday.

They entered a comfortable sitting room just off the main offices, and a small and rather frail old waitress brought coffees and cakes on an ancient trolley which she struggled to control. When she had finally brought it to a quivering stop and handed out the cups, Godfrey began.

'I hope that you're all refreshed after our latish get together on Friday. Since then I've been thinking about you and your future, James, and I have a proposition.'

James leaned forward, alert and eager to hear Godfrey's plan.

Godfrey put down his coffee cup very deliberately, and began to fumble with his pipe and matches, eventually setting them aside and continuing.

'I know that you've seen my old friend Mr. Beloe

recently. And I know that he is keen to offer you a job. Well as it happens, Percival Beloe and I go back a long way - army, the Nomads and so forth - and I think the three of us could come to a very useful and constructive arrangement. I propose that you accept two jobs, not one. You would work for Percival, and you would also work for the Service. Percival could place you in one of his Continental offices where we need more agent handlers, and you could do a splendid job for both of us. Percival's firm does a lot of trade on the Paris Bourse, and as you gathered from Jonathan, Paris is an important location for us, where the trade in information is easily as brisk as the trade on the stock market.'

James was taken aback and had to work hard to stay composed, but he had already decided to accept. 'This sounds extremely interesting, and I'd like to say yes to you Mr. Godfrey, or should I call you Chief?'

'Chief, or head gardener as young Lucinda here calls me. Either will do. Delighted that you think my plan is a good one. In fact I think it's not too early for a celebratory sip of something.' He pressed a bell next to the door, and the aged waitress reappeared.

'Miss Gatt. I wonder if I could impose upon your good nature and ask you to go a step further than coffee duties today by bringing in a tray of sherry please? Something nice and dry and encouraging to the appetite?'

Miss Gatt stood motionless for a moment, fixing Godfrey with a look of frustration and consternation. It seemed that she might flatly refuse his request. Godfrey in turn, was fumbling with his pipe and matches like a crazed juggler.

Eventually Miss Gatt responded slowly, in an icy tone, 'I serve coffees, sir, as you well know. I will make an exception on this one occasion, and on this occasion only.' And with that she withdrew, leaving Godfrey looking a little sheepish.

'Sorry about Miss Gatt. She disapproves of alcohol, and I often suspect she disapproves of me. That was our little ritual which we've performed each day for as long as I can remember. Now where were we? Ah yes - James in Paris! All very good, I think we all agree. But there is something more which I think we can achieve in the short term, and I want to talk about Haldane. Jonathan, I think you'd agree that he's a valuable tool, someone that we would do well to keep close, and look for future opportunities to exploit?'

'Absolutely, Chief,' Jonathan replied, 'He's an established part of the KGB information system. They were very happy for me to pass on the Cyclone data to him. They seem to respect him, or at least they think he's above suspicion. Of course I was never party to who was managing him. Our communication was done at arms length, as you know only too well James, so I don't have any feeling about who he's reporting to. But I do know that in terms of messenger status he's regarded very highly indeed. I'm out of the picture now, but you're just coming into it, James. It would be a good strategic move for you to continue the relationship on some pretext or other.'

There was a loud knocking at the door, and Miss Gatt returned with another, smaller trolley which she manoeuvred with surprising speed and dexterity. She poured out four glasses of a pale fino sherry and handed one to James, Lucinda and Jonathan, with a false obsequiousness which had been perfected over many years. She thrust the fourth glass at Godfrey as if it were scalding her hand, and he grasped it clumsily, a splash of the yellow liquid falling and settling into the wiry material of his jacket. She tottered off without a word, leaving Godfrey looking flushed and rubbing at the stain with his pipe.

'I've seen off the most challenging of foes all round Europe and beyond, but Miss Gatt continues to have the better of me,' he mumbled, half to himself.

'Where were we? Ah yes, we need to keep the door open to Haldane. I believe that he is even more senior in the KBG ranks than we thought. We don't know the identity of his immediate contact in Oxford, but with Komarov wielding a new broom throughout the organisation, I think that there is every chance that he will want to keep Haldane close. And in that case, a relationship with him would leave us only one step away from our main target.'

'There's only one potential problem, Chief,' Jonathan interjected. 'We're assuming that the blame for generating the misinformation on Cyclone will be laid completely at my door. What if they decide that Haldane was somehow complicit, or if they decide that his innocent involvement is worthy of punishment in any case?'

Godfrey looked around the room as if for inspiration, the pale November morning light glinting off his heavy spectacles.

'You have a point, Jonathan. And I suppose we won't have to wait long for an answer to your questions. When is the arms drop, precisely?'

'The early hours of Saturday, Kabul time,' Jonathan replied, 'and given that they're four and a half hours ahead of us, London will know that they've been duped by Saturday morning.'

'So how can we arrange for James to drop in on the old boy on Saturday and make it look like the most natural thing in the world?' Godfrey puzzled.

Lucinda, who until now had been listening approvingly to the proposal to James, stood and walked to the window, her tall figure silhouetted against the grey blue of the winter sky.

'As it happens, Chief, I'm going back to Oxford this weekend. There's a lunch at my old college for graduates - a rather dull networking thing - and I said I'd go along to meet up with a couple of old friends and because I'd nothing better to distract me on Saturday. The other girls will be bringing partners - husbands, boyfriends - that kind of thing. And so James and I could go together, and then he could arrange to drop by Haldane in the evening.'

'What a capital idea, Lucinda,' Godfrey replied, clearly in favour of the plan. 'That's settled then. James, your first mission is to attend a lunch and then have a few drinks. What a rather pleasant way to enter Service life. I only wish that it was always thus.' He grinned as he downed the last of his sherry, a lively good-humour having suddenly taken hold of him. 'Almost time for lunch,' he declared, which also explained his change of mood, 'Must dash. Some odd little tasks to do here before I pop round to The Nomads. Delighted that you're on board, James. I will have Mr. Waft send you the relevant papers tomorrow. Terms and conditions and that sort of dull stuff. And I will see to it that he coordinates with my old chum Percival Beloe. If there's anything new ahead of Saturday, Lucinda can brief you on the way to your lunch.'

Godfrey retreated into his office, and Jonathan, Lucinda and James walked out into the cold. They lingered a while chatting on the steps of Number 9 before Jonathan set off to Charing Cross, and James and Lucinda decided to walk through the park.

'Congratulations, James,' she said as they stood by the fountains, looking north to where the Palace's grey facade glinted in the weak sun. 'I told you that Godfrey liked your manner. And the Paris station. It's very smart indeed. I've visited them a couple of times and they're a good team. You'll get along well with Francois and his people, and it's a very busy office so you'll have plenty of work. Do you know the city at all?'

'Not really. I spent a week there one summer looking round the galleries. Took a bus and ferry and hung out in youth hostels near the Gare du Nord. How about you?'

'Yes indeed. We have a small flat in the Avenue Montaigne. Very pretty and ridiculously expensive. I like to sit at the cafe next to Alma Marceau and watch the people go by. Sometimes I take a trip on the Bateaux-Mouches and explore the city that way.'

'Always on your own. You seem to be happy in your own company, but that's lucky for us I guess, since it means you didn't already have a companion for the lunch on Saturday.'

'If you're asking about men James, then I have to admit that I find them immeasurably disappointing. Most men I meet just want to talk about themselves; they are utter bores. And they take one look at me and think - sex. Their brains seem to short circuit at the sight of me. You know, it was really interesting to experience the indifference that I encountered from men when I was the frumpy Sue Almond.'

'I hope you don't think that I was one of them!'

'Not at all, James. You were the exception. Most men seemed to assume that I was dim. Which is rich when many of the dimmest of men seem to think that they're intellectually superior to all women. I think that's why I enjoy life so much in the Service. At work I can be myself. I'm respected for my brains and because I can look after myself. And because people like Godfrey and Jonathan are so focused on getting results, it's meant that I've risen up the ranks very quickly. There's a lot of mutual respect in the department. Take Harry for instance. Very good at his job, but he knows that I'm a lot smarter than him.'

'I get the impression that Harry wouldn't want to mess with you, Lucinda. He seems a little in awe of you.'

'Interesting observation. He's intelligent and courteous. In fact, he's a real gentleman.'

They walked north towards the entrance to Green Park, skirting round the groups of tourists who had braved the cold to watch the guards in the Palace forecourt.

'I respect all of that,' James said eventually, 'I just meant, isn't it good to have company? To have someone to share things with sometimes?'

'Of course, James.' She paused, and then continued, 'I suppose that I do get a bit lonely at times if I'm honest. Last summer I booked into a suite at the Excelsior Vittoria in Sorrento and just sat about on the terrace watching the couples in their own worlds. I suppose that the job does get in the way of any kind of relationship. It's not easy to keep up the pretence of going to an ordinary office every day. I guess that so far I've just not met the right guy in the right circumstances.'

They had reached the tube station opposite The Ritz and they faced each other for a moment.

'Lucinda,' James started, 'Can I just say something personal?'

'Of course', she replied, uncertainly.

'What are you doing over Christmas? If you're going back to Scotland, I'd like you to visit me at my folks' place in Glasgow. If you're hanging about at a loose end, it would make a bit of a change. Although it's not exactly the Excelsior Vittoria.'

Lucinda brightened and laughed. 'You know, James, that would be delightful. I'd like to meet your parents and hear all your Dad's stories first hand. Let's do that.'

They sat together silently on the tube heading north, both smiling up at the adverts above the seats. At Warren Street James rose to change lines and Lucinda called out,

'See you at Marylebone at nine o'clock on Saturday, James. Wear your suit, and look smart. I don't want my date to let me down.'

She grinned at him as he stepped off the train, and he smiled back as the doors closed, and Lucinda Latham was propelled north towards the Angel.

# CHAPTER 12 THE AGE OF INNOCENCE

Letters signed by Beloe and Waft confirming James's new roles arrived at South Grove two days later. From the phone box in Pond Square he called Haldane to arrange to visit that weekend. Haldane was in good spirits, and readily agreed to meet before dinner. Digging out more coins, he dialled Glasgow to tell them his good news.

'Listen to this Maggie,' he could hear his father calling through the house. 'He's got a job doing broking, and he says he's moving to Paris. Can you credit that?'

'Not right away, Dad,' James corrected, 'I have to do some training in the West End first. And there's more news which I'll fill you in on when I'm home for Christmas. Another bit of work I'll be doing for the Foreign Office. Oh, and while I remember, I'd like to bring a friend home to visit at Christmas. She's called Lucinda.'

'Lucinda? That's an odd name. Don't you mean Lucy?'

'No its Lucinda, Dad. Lucinda Latham.'

He could hear George turn again to his mother,

'He's talking about a job, and a girlfriend.'

George turned back to the phone, and with a laugh he continued, 'This Latham girl, she wouldn't by any chance be related to Lord Latham?'

'One of his daughters, Dad. And she's looking forward to meeting you both.'

'Good grief, James. An honest job, and marrying into the aristocracy. It's a lot for us to take in at once. Of course we'll be pleased to meet her.'

'I think you're getting a little ahead of events, Dad. We're just friends. We met...,' he paused as he realised how complicated this could become, '...in London. At a restaurant.'

'Well we look forward to hearing all your news when you're up next month. Congratulations once again.'

James wandered back to South Grove. His thoughts were already turning to his next meeting with Lucinda.

Saturday came around quickly, and James found himself under the arch at Marylebone, eagerly awaiting her arrival. She stepped out of a cab just before nine and regarded him approvingly - his suit cleaned, gleaming shoes, new tie. 'You'll do', she quipped as they headed to the platform. Under her Jaeger cashmere coat she was wearing a Ralph Lauren blazer, white t-shirt, and designer jeans tucked into ankle boots. James liked the style and said so.

'It's informal and I'm comfortable in it, James. A lot of the serious alumni of Lady Hillary Hall will be in a depressing array of the most frumpy outfits. God, I hope this lunch isn't too ghastly.'

'I'm sure it'll be fine,' he replied, hopefully.

'You haven't met my dear contemporaries yet, James. After twenty minutes you'll be considering defenestration as an attractive option.'

The carriage was empty, and she talked about some of the darker aspects of her role in counter-intelligence, and the methods used by the KGB's so-called executive action group in eliminating internal dissidents and foreign threats. These 'liquid affairs' as they called them were a terrifying reminder of the lengths to which the other side would go to in order to maintain the status quo amongst their own people. Komarov was now the most feared power within the organisation.

'Would you be able to identify him?' James asked. 'Do we think he ever operates in the UK ?'

'Jonathan and MG have briefed me about him, and yes, he does sometimes work here under assumed identities. He's about the same age as the Chief, but different in every other way. Tall, athletic, good head of hair, and a distinct lack of milk bottle glasses.'

'And what do you think about what we're actually doing here? I understand that one has to be completely in, or out of the Service - there's no half way house. But what are the ethical arguments for Operation Cyclone? What's your take on it all?'

'You're right James. Our life is like a military

one. You have to follow the policy makers' decisions and just get on with it. But I do have a clear view of what we're doing in Afghanistan. The Marxist government was a shambles. The Afghan people were being tortured and killed, and countless numbers were starving. Then the Russians invaded, but mainly because they saw a risk that the Afghan government might side with the US. And now the oppression of the hapless Afghan people continues, only under a new set of brutal thugs.

'So where do you see it going? How will it end?'

'My hope, James, is that with our help, the insurgents will turn this war into a long act of attrition, at the end of which, the Soviet military will be weakened, and discredited. It may even play a part in the ultimate collapse of the Soviet State.

'My fear, on the other hand, is that we can't control the people we're helping to arm; we're helping some very dangerous people to make war. That's fine as long as they share our beliefs, and this all leads to setting up a democracy. But I worry that we might unwittingly be playing the role of Dr. Frankenstein.'

The train was drawing into the station. They picked up their bags and stepped down onto the platform.

'To answer your question, James. I don't think it will end. I wish I did, but I don't.'

They had plenty of time ahead of the lunch, so they wandered along St Giles enjoying the cold winter air. It was forecast to snow later and the sky was beginning to fill with milky clouds. They were staying the night at The Old Rectory, one of the best hotels in Oxford, which Lucinda always used on visits. She received an effusive welcome from the reception team who insisted on giving her and James the two best rooms on the top floor. James waited patiently by the open fire as she exchanged notes with the staff about the other guests. She had such a disarming manner, and he was taken aback by how much she was able to learn in such a short time.

Their rooms faced each other off a narrow corridor in the eaves. James was impressed by how spacious his room was, and tried not to think too much about the cost which was more than he had ever paid for a hotel room.

They had agreed to meet just before noon and left their rooms at exactly the same time. They found themselves pressed together as they descended in the small, softly-lit lift. They were so close that he could smell her perfume.

'We're very close,' he muttered.

'Indeed. You're standing on my foot,' she replied.

'I meant our rooms are very close,' he continued, moving his foot awkwardly.

'And your point is?'

'Just very handy in case we want a nightcap later on when we're finished with Haldane.'

'Look, James. We're professionals, and we both

know that it would be complicated for us to, umm - she seemed to hesitate - get much closer, especially if we're working in the same department.'

'But I'll be in Paris,' he continued.

He leaned a little closer to her, but as he did, the lift doors opened and she set off through the hall, calling back with a laugh,

'Let's just see how things go this evening, James. Don't distract me just now. I have to concentrate on the harridans of Hillary.'

It was a short walk to Lucinda's college and as they approached the porter's lodge she gripped his arm and started.

'Oh fuck! It's that two-faced bitch, Richenda Sumption. She's absolutely appalling. Try to steer well clear of her, James. She's a nightmare. Oh Christ, she's coming over here!'

'Richenda! How wonderful to see you again! It's been far too long, darling,' Lucinda greeted the newcomer with an air kiss.

The woman was tall and thin, and James found himself thinking of a painting he'd seen in Paris by Otto Dix, of a tall and angular woman. Richenda might have modelled herself on the painting; she wore her high-necked red and black checked dress and held her sobranie in a languorous pose. Her short hair was cut in a manly style. All that she lacked to complete the look was a large monocle.

'Lucinda. Didn't expect to see you here. Thought this might be a bit serious for you. How's office life?

How're you coping with the routine? Remind me, what is it that you do again?'

'Office administration, Richenda, at the Foreign Office. Not a lot to say about it really, to be honest.'

'Waste of a decent brain, if you ask me. You were reasonably bright as far as I recall. Although it's only now that I'm teaching here that I understand what real intellect is. Our undergraduate days were a mere prelude to the serious understanding of our subjects.'

'And how *are* your studies on the punctuation in Milton's later works coming along, Richenda? I must say, they sound fascinating.'

The androgynous figure ignored Lucinda and turned to James.

'Who's this?'

'James Gunn,' Lucinda stepped in before James could reply. 'He's accompanying me today as he has a short break from his lecture tour on the English essayists. He's terribly self-effacing. He wouldn't dream of mentioning his potential seat at Cambridge, or the astounding advance he's had from the OUP for his thesis on something or other. Isn't that right, James dearest?'

Richenda peered at James briefly, grunted huffily, and then retreated without further comment, leaving Lucinda in a state of sheer elation.

'God, that was good,' she said under her breath, and then a thought struck her.

'Beware James, the only woman here who's more

painful than Richenda is the vile Camilla Crowley. Dreadful woman - so vulgar. Try to avoid being sat next to her at all costs.'

They made their way into the dining hall and stood around chatting as the old friends caught up with the news of their new lives and careers. James kept one eye on Richenda, making sure that she was out of earshot so that he could tell the truth about his own story, which he confined to the job at Leclerc Proust. He enjoyed the company and it soon became obvious to him that as Lucinda's partner, he was the object of much attention and speculation. Lucinda introduced him to her old friends Kay and Aileen, who showed a keen interest in how they'd met and how long they'd known each other.

Kay took Lucinda to one side. 'It's so nice to see you, Lucy. Now that I'm stuck into my research degree I hardly ever get a chance to get back to Oxford and I never get to London. What I don't understand from your letters is just why your job's so all-consuming, when against all advice, you've chosen to work in lowly office admin? You never seem to have any time off, and I've given up any hope of you having the time to visit me in Nottingham.'

'The admin. just keeps piling up, and in many ways it's my own fault, Kay. I'm not nearly organised enough. But I promise I'll take the train up to see you in the Spring, or perhaps on my way to Scotland at Christmas.'

'That would be fantastic, Lucy,' Kay replied. 'And

what about James? I had no idea you had a boyfriend. You've never even mentioned him before. I have to say, Lucy, he's very good-looking, and he doesn't seem to realise it. I like that - it makes a very refreshing change. Tell me that you're serious about him. You'd be a fool not to be.'

Lucinda couldn't suppress a smile. 'I suppose he's not too bad.'

'Speaks volumes.' Kay replied, as she rejoined the group.

The butler called for them to take their seats, and Lucinda steered James towards the long table in the centre of the medieval dining hall, which was beautifully laid, each plate adorned with the three red stars of the college crest.

Suddenly there was a commotion behind them and a tall woman in an orange dress pushed forward.

'Well I say! Who's this, Lucinda? I don't believe that we've been introduced. Come. Sit next to Henry and me.' The woman grabbed James's hand and ushered him into a chair next to her own. 'Camilla Crowley, James. Delighted to meet you. I want to know all about you and how long you and young Lucinda have been *a deux*.'

James soon found that they had exchanged the intellectual snobs for their social equivalents.

'You came by train, Lucinda. How quaint. Henry drove us here in his Rover. We're going on to Bellingham Manor tonight. A friend of Henry who's in metals bought it last year. It's probably as big as your Daddy's place in Scotland. Such very impressive grounds, and real cattle.'

'Leclerc Proust you say, Jamie old chap?' Henry boomed, his red face and red hair clashing horribly with his pink trousers and yellow and blue checked tweeds. 'You'll never make any serious money in a place like that you know. You need to get into commodities, old boy. And all this college stuff. What's the point of any of it? Look at me. No qualifications to speak of, but now I'm earning enough to buy out anyone around this table - old money as well as new.'

'Well that's quite an achievement, Henry', James replied, 'but perhaps life can be about more than just money.' And looking across at Lucinda, he continued,

What about culture, values - style? Can money buy those things, or don't they matter?

Henry was already bored with the conversation, and was frantically looking around the table for another bottle of claret.

'Whatever you say, James old fruit. All a bit philosophical for me. Let's crack open another Pomerol or, mark my words, I'll die of thirst!'

Meanwhile, Camilla was keen to understand exactly how their relationship had come about.

'We met in a restaurant in Covent Garden, and we hit it off right away. We're both Scottish, and we both like the same kind of things.' Lucinda started.

'And your family, James. Do they have land in Scotland? What do they do?'

'Of course,' James replied quickly, before Lucinda could interject, and in conspiratorial tones continued. 'We like to fly a little under the radar, as it were, Camilla. You won't find anything about the family in the newspapers. We're very discreet. Just let's say that we're talking west of Scotland, with some serious military connections. And I'm afraid we'll have to leave it at that.' He leaned closer to Camilla, his eyes deep pools of sincerity. 'I could tell you a lot more, but then you'd be compromised, and I couldn't live with the consequences.'

Camilla was thrilling to James's attention, and was leering a little drunkenly. 'I love your accent, James. You are a very intriguing young man. I think that being compromised by you might be quite pleasurable.'

Lucinda frowned uncomfortably across at them trying to hear the threads of their conversation, but as Camilla reached for the wine James winked at her, as if to say, "You're not the only one adept at deflection and bullshit". Lucinda smiled back at him, and for a moment, the chatter of the lunch table receded into the background.

As the wine began to take effect, Camilla and Henry drifted slowly into a state of inebriation, receding as they did so into the background of the conversation. James found himself enjoying the optimistic talk around the table of new jobs and new starts. He could see that Lucinda too, was relaxing, and by mid-afternoon as the last glasses of port were emptied, the coffee cups cleared away and the lunch party began to disperse, she and James were both feeling quite mellow.

As they collected their coats and said their good-byes, snow started falling on the grass of the quad, collecting around the ivy-clad walls of the dining hall. As they made their way back along St Giles, quickening their steps as the snow fell in increasing flurries, the cold air cleared their heads and they began to rehearse James's lines ahead of the meeting with Haldane. They had an hour to kill before James was due to meet him in his rooms, and he had arranged to see Dave and some old friends for a quick drink in the college bar before the encounter. James suggested that Lucinda accompany him to the drinks and also to meet Haldane. It would help to present a consistent picture, and having another potential line into Haldane seemed like a sensible idea. Lucinda liked the idea, and held on to his arm as the snow began to form a slippery carpet on the pavements.

When they arrived at St. Gabriel's they headed straight to the cellar bar, where the atmosphere was thick with smoke and the steam rising from the rows of wet coats which lined the damp walls. Dave pushed through the crowd, a broad grin on his face.

'James. Great to see you! Good grief - who's this?

You look far too classy for a skinny mongrel like our Jamie.' And with this, he grabbed James in a headlock, which was obviously meant as a playful gesture, but to the uninitiated looked like a serious assault. James kept an eye on Lucinda's handbag, and for a crazed moment he imagined her pulling out her Walther to take charge of the proceedings.

'Steady, Dave,' James struggled upright. 'This is Lucinda. A friend from London.'

'Not one of your more informative statements, James.' Dave responded, feigning despair.

'Lucinda - welcome. Let me buy you a drink. Come this way to the bar and I'll introduce you to the crowd.'

James was left to hang up their coats, but was soon catching up on the latest college gossip with Phil. He had been giving some thought to Haldane's handler. Haldane must meet with countless social contacts every week; students, visiting academics, the college board of trustees, contacts from his old life in Whitehall. There were any number of connections and contacts which would seem like natural entries in his busy diary.

'Has Haldane been very visible recently?' he asked Phil, 'I mean, have there been any special visitors and dinners - that kind of thing?'

'Just the usual dinners for this time of year,' Phil replied, 'Haldane spends a lot of his time with the students - he's really popular with all the years - and of course he's writing a book on some history or other I think. I'm a bit vague on that. But no - life just ticks along as usual, with Haldane presiding over dinners, and his right-hand man always at his elbow and ready to fill his glass.'

Always at his elbow. His right-hand man. It was suddenly obvious to James; it was the other way around. Haldane was working for Pringle! He was always there, hiding in plain sight. And those arguments and altercations which he had overheard. It wasn't wine and dinners that they'd been arguing over. It all began to become very clear.

But then James was jolted out of his thoughts by a cacophony of laughter at the bar, and he could see Lucinda leaning against the brass counter, pint of Guinness in hand, encircled by an admiring group hanging on her every word. She was playing the part of an urbane and wealthy enigma, locked in a ludicrous office environment of pointless activity and preposterous characters. Dave and the group were enthralled, and as he approached, James could see the growing hero worship in the eyes of the undergraduate girls as they compared Lucinda's tailored and expensive look to their own assorted jeans and leggings.

Dave spotted James and drew him to one side.

'She's fantastic, Jamie. So witty, and a mind like a bloody razor. I know she's having a laugh now, but we had a serious chat earlier about her degree, the teaching here, what was good, what should be improved. I'd like to pick her brains in future. That's assuming that you two are actually a couple. It all seemed a bit vague earlier.'

'It's early days, Dave, but we'll definitely be seeing each other one way or another. You know, I have to admit that I'm feeling a bit smitten. I mean, I like her a lot.'

Dave looked at him knowingly. 'Look. Just so that you can relax James, you should know that she told me everything.'

'She did?', James rocked back a little, willing him to continue.

'Absolutely everything. How you met in Covent Garden, how you were very kind to her before you found out that she's bloody loaded. How she feels she can talk to you about her work - which, by the way sounds like the most boring job on God's earth. The only thing about Lucy which I don't get is the job. She could do so much better without even trying. But there we are, Jamie. I know all about you two. Scotland. The trip to your folks next month. The whole story. From what she says, I think you'll definitely be seeing a lot more of Lucy!'

'So it's Lucy is it? Very familiar, I'm sure.' James responded with a great sense of relief. 'Well I must admit you seem to have the complete picture, Dave. There's not a lot more that I can add.'

'And she has a great sense of humour, Jamie. It may seem strange to you, but some of her stories - they remind me of the funny tales that your old colleague Sue used to recount. You obviously tend to go for the same kind of girls, Jamie.'

'Indeed. I'm sure you have a good point there.' James replied, keen to move the conversation on. And noticing the time, he walked back to the bar where he prised Lucinda from her new friends, and they began to gather their coats to make the visit to Haldane.

'How long will your meeting take, James?' Dave asked. 'Why don't we all meet up later for dinner?'

'We'd love to, David,' Lucinda replied readily. 'An excellent idea. We're at the Old Rectory, so anywhere near there would be just perfect. I'll leave the arrangements in your experienced gourmet's hands.'

'Right you are then.' Dave exploded with delight. 'Next stop dinner!'

James and Lucinda made their way through the crowd and up the narrow steps which led to the front quad. The time had come for the purpose of their visit. They both felt a warmth in each other's company but as the cold of the night air and the falling snow hit them as they surfaced from the cellars, their thoughts also hardened and chilled, for in a few moments they would know Haldane's fate.

# CHAPTER 13 THE GOOD SOLDIER

As they reached the front quad the storm was becoming more intense, and they could just make out the outlines of students hurrying to reach the shelter of the dining hall against the swirling screen of snow. James put his arm around Lucinda, guiding her to the porter's lodge, where they could stay out of the icy blast long enough to decide how they would approach Haldane. James also wanted to share his thoughts about Pringle. They huddled just inside the lodge, next to the mail pigeonholes.

'I think I have a good idea of who Haldane's been passing our information on to,' James began, 'so I reckon I might know his superior. On several occasions I've heard Haldane and the college butler arguing in a way that just doesn't seem right now that I look back on it. And I suppose that the butler comes and goes from here without anyone taking much notice.'

Lucinda considered this. 'OK. So if he happens to be with Haldane when we go to his rooms, we should be careful to stick to our script. You're thrilled about your new job in Paris. You're going to stay in touch with MG. So from Haldane's perspective, you might be a useful source of intelligence in future. As for me, I have a fairly low-level job in the Foreign Office, and so once again, he'll see me as someone who might be a useful source in future. We don't overplay our hand. We just tell him how happy we are, and we make it clear that we're in a relationship.'

'How do we do the last bit?' James asked.

'Why don't we try just being ourselves, Jamie?' she replied with a laugh. 'I don't think that we need a script for that part.'

'And of course this is all dependent on Pringle - or whoever is pulling his strings - deciding that Haldane is in the clear over the Operation Cyclone debacle,' she added.

James was about to turn back out of the lodge, when suddenly Lucinda grabbed the back of his head and pulled him towards her. Their lips met, and he wrapped his arms around her snow-covered overcoat. She pulled him closer, and they stepped back against the shelves of mail, sending letters and parcels sliding to the floor in a storm of paper which echoed the falling snow outside.

Then just as suddenly she pushed him back, and beckoning to him, darted towards the college gates where she carefully looked out through the snow into Turl Street.

'That was nice.' James whispered.

'That was necessary.' Lucinda replied. She

pointed to a large Mercedes, where a tall man in an overcoat and a large black homburg was being ushered into the back seat by a burly-looking minder.

'Komarov.' She said. 'I caught sight of him out of the corner of my eye, and had to make sure that he didn't see our faces. James - if he's been to visit your old rector friend, then I fear that it wasn't for reasons of social pleasantries. This doesn't feel good.'

'In that case' - James started back into the front quad - 'let's get round to his rooms now and try to find out why Komarov was here.'

Back into the snow they went, walking briskly now, their breath mingling with the white air. Half way up Haldane's staircase James paused.

'Let me go in first, just to make sure everything's OK. Then I'll come and fetch you in a couple of minutes and then I can make the introductions.'

Lucinda waited on a bench seat while James sprinted up the final flight of steps to the Rector's rooms. As he was about to knock, he noticed a thin yellow slit of light in the doorway. The door was ajar. He moved forward stealthily, and pushed the door open as quietly as he could. The room was dimly-lit. Only the desk lamp shed any light, picking out the papers and charts piled on the surface, with the phone, the paperweight and the paper knife all in their familiar places. As James's eyes became accustomed to the half light, he could see the shapes of the paintings and prints, the vibrant colours of the Kandinsky now reduced to browns and dark reds.

And then he saw the long shadow cast against the painting, which moved almost imperceptibly, a little way, side to side. It was the shadow of a man. And only then as he peered through the gloom, did he see the body suspended from the ceiling beam, its feet swaying ever so slightly, its lifeless fingers stretched out as if in some final grasp for life, its neck broken and twisted at a grotesque angle. A college tie had been entwined around the rope, its blue stripes just visible as James stared in horror towards the ceiling.

James fought to control his shock, and tried to think about what steps to take. Would he find a suicide note amongst the papers on the desk? Or had Haldane's death been staged to look like suicide? It was just then that he realised that there was no chair or stool around the body. And Haldane couldn't have stepped off the desk which was several feet away. He moved forward, the ancient floorboards creaking under his feet, and in that instant, just as he realised that this was indeed a murder scene, he was suddenly aware of a shape bursting from the back room and launching itself towards him. As James turned, the assailant caught him with a blow to the side of his head, and he staggered backwards. As he reached out to break his fall, he grasped at the surface of the desk, only succeeding in pulling bundles of papers down on top of him.

He looked up from his position on the floor between the desk and the chesterfield and tried to make out the figure of his attacker, but he was unable to focus. As the man advanced menacingly towards him, James tried to clear his mind and coordinate his movements, but he was struggling to maintain consciousness.

And then he was dimly aware of another figure in the room. It was Lucinda, who had heard the sound of him crashing to the floor, and was now behind the man, who had turned and was trying to wrestle something out of her hand. James could just make out the silhouette of her gun, as they crashed against the bookcase, and the heavily-set figure used his full weight to crush her against its doors. He heard the crack of glass and then of wood as he bore down upon her.

The scene swam in and out of his sight. James fought back a rising panic. His head throbbed and his legs were leaden, but he told himself that he had to focus. A confusion of images flashed through his mind. Godfrey was staring blankly at him. Haldane was pouring a sherry. He was visiting his father in hospital. And now he was back at school. And he was in the playground, and he was cornered. But now he was calm and composed. His fingers felt Haldane's long silver paper knife which had fallen to the floor. He could feel the raised college crest on the handle. His fist closed around it, his thumb firmly pressed over the end. Then drawing on every reserve of energy, he rose and straightening quickly, he swung his right hand through the air of the study with all his force, driving the sharpened point into the attacker's neck.

The assailant loosened his grip on Lucinda who fell to the floor. He stood motionless, silently clawing at the knife and then in a frenzied panic he turned towards James, arms flailing. James stepped aside, and with a sharp kick to his ribs sent him crashing backwards on to the chesterfield.

James helped Lucinda to her feet and she motioned to him that she was OK. He moved to the doorway, still holding Lucinda around her waist, and flicked on the light switch.

Haldane's body was motionless now, his figure casting a long shadow across the floor of the study. James and Lucinda stepped forward, and now they were able to see their attacker clearly. The paper knife had severed the carotid artery, and the red leather chesterfield was awash with blood. The dead eyes of the man he knew as Alexander Pringle stared ahead as if fixed on the print of the battle scene which hung behind them.

James held Lucinda closer, as the blood began to drip to the floor and form a dark and expanding pool.

Lucinda pushed her hair out of her eyes and turned to him.

'Welcome to the Service, James,' she said. 'You've found that place you've been looking for. There's no going back now.'

He looked beyond the chaos of the room and out of the leaded windows to where the snow was falling steadily, creating a blanket of silence around the college. He bent down and picked up Lucinda's pistol, which had fallen during the struggle. His father had told him that he would make a difference, that he would sort out the world's problems with his brain, and not with a gun. But why not with both?

He slipped the gun into his jacket pocket. An unfamiliar feeling of self-confidence stirred within him. He felt in control. He turned, smiling, to Lucinda.

'I've arrived, Lucy' he replied, '..and it feels like home.'

# ACKNOWLEDGEMENTS

Many thanks to Beth for editing, and for her suggestions and support.

Thanks also to Jamie, David and Nadia for the cover photograph.

Printed in Great Britain
by Amazon

70466445R00119